Gunfire  e door

Bullets smas̲h̲e̲d̲ t̲h̲r̲o̲u̲g̲h̲ t̲h̲e̲ thin plasterboard and the window glass behind the desk. The gathering storm chose that moment to unleash its fury. Great sheets of rain washed down over the city.

Wu glanced out the broken window, the wind blowing her red-dyed hair into wilder disarray. "We're not jumping," she said fearfully.

"No," Bolan replied. "We're going up." He stepped in beside her, keeping his body against hers so if she made a move to get another weapon he'd know. "You've got to trust me."

"Trust you? Mister, I don't even know who the hell you are."

"I'm the guy who saved your life."

Another hail of bullets knocked chunks from the door. "At least," the soldier said, "I've saved your life so far." He drew the Beretta, leaned out the window and fired a triburst at the sixth-floor window above them.

MACK BOLAN ®
The Executioner

DON PENDLETON'S

EXECUTIONER®

THE

DEADLY PURSUIT

The
Moon Shadow
Trilogy
Book II

A GOLD EAGLE BOOK FROM

W❊RLDWIDE®

TORONTO • NEW YORK • LONDON
AMSTERDAM • PARIS • SYDNEY • HAMBURG
STOCKHOLM • ATHENS • TOKYO • MILAN
MADRID • WARSAW • BUDAPEST • AUCKLAND

First edition August 2003
ISBN 0-373-64297-0

Special thanks and acknowledgment to
Mel Odom for his contribution to this work.

DEADLY PURSUIT

...in the course of justice, none of us
Should see salvation: we do pray for mercy,
And that same prayer doth teach us all to render
The deeds of mercy.

> —William Shakespeare
> *The Merchant of Venice, IV, i, 184*

My brand of justice leaves little room for mercy.
If you do the crime, expect to pay the price—
permanently.

> —Mack Bolan

THE
MACK BOLAN®
LEGEND

Nothing less than a war could have fashioned the destiny of the man called Mack Bolan. Bolan earned the Executioner title in the jungle hell of Vietnam.

But this soldier also wore another name—Sergeant Mercy. He was so tagged because of the compassion he showed to wounded comrades-in-arms and Vietnamese civilians.

Mack Bolan's second tour of duty ended prematurely when he was given emergency leave to return home and bury his family, victims of the Mob. Then he declared a one-man war against the Mafia.

He confronted the Families head-on from coast to coast, and soon a hope of victory began to appear. But Bolan had broken society's every rule. That same society started gunning for this elusive warrior—to no avail.

So Bolan was offered amnesty to work within the system against terrorism. This time, as an employee of Uncle Sam, Bolan became Colonel John Phoenix. With a command center at Stony Man Farm in Virginia, he and his new allies—Able Team and Phoenix Force—waged relentless war on a new adversary: the KGB.

But when his one true love, April Rose, died at the hands of the Soviet terror machine, Bolan severed all ties with Establishment authority.

Now, after a lengthy lone-wolf struggle and much soul-searching, the Executioner has agreed to enter an "arm's-length" alliance with his government once more, reserving the right to pursue personal missions in his Everlasting War.

Prologue

Shanghai, China, 1853

"War is breaking out! An army marches to Shanghai! Soon, my friends, you will be free!"

His face covered in sweat, his back aching from long hours of manual labor, and knowing that hours of hard work yet remained, Mushu Zhao glanced at the speaker with little real curiosity and no hope for the things that were promised. Talk of bloody revenge against the hated British, Americans and French had passed through Shanghai's docks for months.

"Go away," Minh-Quan roared. "We are honest men working honest jobs. We want to hear none of your talk about wars."

"You're fools, then." The speaker was squat and broad, and he had the look of a man well fed. His dark blue robes carried road dust but were well kept. He wore a short sword at his side.

The stranger didn't belong among the overworked men who filled Shanghai's docks. The dockworkers labored every day from morning's first light until the ships' captains and merchants no longer wished to light lanterns at night. Their whole lives could be spent on the wooden docks that stabbed into the turgid brown waters of the Whangpu River. And after all that hard work, they barely made enough money to feed their families. They watched in sorrow as sons stepped into the same jobs their fathers had and daughters turned to prostitution to service the foreigners.

Anger stirred inside Mushu. He quelled the emotion, because he knew the impulse came from his father's family, passed down through the generations. The Zhao family had struggled for more than fifty years, and even before the momentous life of Chi-Kan Zhao, the family hadn't done well.

"I'm no fool," Minh-Quan replied, pulling himself up to his full height. Years of working the docks had left him massively muscled. Even the English and British taskmasters managing the warehouses and ships steered clear of him.

Automatically the stranger among the dockworkers dropped his right hand to the sword hilt.

"Minh-Quan," old Pi-Ao whispered, clutching at the man's elbow. Pi-Ao was a thin stork of a man with gray hair and a hollow face. "Come away from this man. I beg you."

Instead, Minh-Quan stood his ground as Mushu knew he would. Minh-Quan didn't earn the respect he had by backing down.

The clangor of bells and the harsh noise of men's voices rang out along the docks. There was never a time when the docks were silent.

Dark emotion swirled in the stranger's eyes, then disappeared. He took his hand from the weapon. "Minh-Quan," he said in silken tones, "perhaps you are an honest man working an honest job, but you are not paid an honest wage."

"It is the best that is offered."

"It is little more than poverty wages. And there are others

who do not do as well as you." The stranger waved toward the river where the ships stood at anchor, all awaiting loading or unloading. Dockworkers marched across gangplanks like ants. "The foreign devils make the true profit. They only pass on the leavings that they know they can't keep for themselves."

Several men in the group of dockworkers mumbled agreements. Overhead, the boom arm bearing a loaded cargo net swung toward the dock and started to lower. Crates and barrels strained against the net, promising more backbreaking labor.

Along the coast, Mushu knew, the ocean at least offered cooling breezes. He longed for the ocean, but he knew that his father had moved them from there in an effort to step beyond their past. Shanghai held a chance to start over where no one knew much about them, and no one remembered that the Zhao family was once pirates.

"The outsiders reap the profits of our pain," the stranger went on. "They deal with India, and ship the damn opium that steals the lives from our people even though the emperor has outlawed the product."

Mushu knew that was true. If not for the British, French and Americans, China couldn't have gotten the illegal drug in such quantities. As things stood now, the country was drowning in opium. Dens promoting the drug's usage lined the harbor and reached deeply into Chinese City, as well as the international settlement, where the foreigners lived in grand style.

"There is no other way for us to live," a calm voice said.

The dockworkers and the stranger turned to face the new speaker. Mushu recognized his father.

Tsun-Chung Zhao was in his early forties, more than twice Mushu's nineteen years. His right cheek held a dimple that was the result of a pistol ball fired into his face when he was younger than his son. He wore the khaki trousers and white shirt sold in stores the warehousemen owned, taking back the pitiful wages they paid the laborers.

The cargo net descended nearby. When the crates and barrels thudded against the dock, a shiver traveled through the platform.

"There are other ways," the stranger insisted.

"How?" Tsun-Chung challenged. "By standing against the invaders?"

The stranger's eyes hardened. "Would you be a dog for them, Tsun-Chung Zhao?"

Tsun-Chung stood straighter then, and Mushu's heart swelled with pride.

"If you know me, then you know I am no man's dog."

"Yet," the stranger said, "here I find you dressed in clothes the invaders have provided their coolie laborers."

Tsun-Chung's bullet-dimpled cheek jumped, and Mushu knew from experience that his father was about to lose his temper. "You come perilously close," he admonished in a cold, calm voice, "to disrespect."

The stranger bowed, pushing his arms out to either side but never taking his eyes from Tsun-Chung. "I mean no disrespect. I seek only to speak the truth."

"The British and the Americans have powerful weapons," Tsun-Chung said, nodding to one of the passing gunboats the British manned. The red, white and blue Union Jack flew proudly from the bow, and sunlight glinted from the cannon.

"We have more men," the stranger said.

"Not all men work together."

"But we can," the stranger entreated. "We have begun organizing—"

Tsun-Chung spit. "You are children playing at warriors."

The stranger's face hardened. "We are freedom fighters. Soon, all of the white devils will fear us."

"They will hunt you down," Tsun-Chung said in a sad

voice, "and they will kill you. In turn, you will get others killed."

"If I were not looking at you," the stranger stated, "I would swear that I was talking to an old woman."

Tsun-Chung took a step forward, and Mushu knew that the encounter could only end in blood between the two men. His father was a man unused to disrespect. Automatically Mushu strode forward, intending to aid his father.

A whistle blasted.

Mushu turned, spotting the seven Britons in crisp khakis approaching with haste.

"What is going on here?" the British officer demanded in clipped English. He held a heavy Adams revolver in one white-gloved hand.

As was his nature, Tsun-Chung addressed the British officer, speaking for all of them. Although he'd traveled to Shanghai to live a quiet life and to escape the violence of his family's pirating past, he couldn't evade his own nature to take command. Leaders were born, Mushu had often heard, and his father lived true to a long legacy of leaders.

A passing rickshaw pulled to a halt. Another Briton, this one easily in his late sixties, sat with a young prostitute on his arm. The man was white haired and hatchet-faced. The hawk's beak of a nose was the centerpiece to harsh features. His suit showed elegance and wealth in every well-tailored line.

"A minor disagreement," Tsun-Chung said in perfect English. Most of the dockworkers usually pretended to have only a rudimentary understanding of the foreign language.

"There'll be no disagreements on my watch," the British officer stated, bristling.

Tsun-Chung tilted his head and bowed. "My apologies, Major."

"It's sergeant. Sergeant Beckworth."

Mushu knew his father had made a deliberate mistake to play to the Briton's ego.

"Of course." Tsun-Chung made a sweeping bow. "I will see that these men get back to work."

"Chop-chop," the sergeant growled. "Bloody chop-chop."

"Sergeant! Detain that man!" The order came from the well-dressed man in the rickshaw.

The sergeant glared at the man.

"You'd bloody well better carry out that order, Sergeant Beckworth," the old man snarled, "or I'll have your stripes and your arse for my troubles. I'm Admiral Horace Cauling, late of Her Majesty's Royal Navy." His tone carried a familiarity with command.

"Of course, Admiral." Beckworth gestured, and his men sprang forward with their muskets at the ready. Two men grabbed Tsun-Chung and pulled him forward while the others drove the dockworkers back.

Mushu stared helplessly at his father.

"Step back, boy," Tsun-Chung ordered in their native tongue.

The stranger moved forward smoothly, drawing the attention of the British soldiers. He roped a hand around Mushu's chest and pulled him back.

"Come with me, boy," the stranger whispered. "Come with me if you want to live."

Horrified, Mushu watched the old admiral climb from the rickshaw and shrug out of the young prostitute's arms. He crossed the dock to Tsun-Chung, then pulled down Tsun-Chung's left sleeve.

The tattoo of the full moon obscured by clouds stood out in bold relief against the inside of Tsun-Chung's forearm.

Cauling grinned coldly in triumph. "Do you know the significance of this mark, Sergeant?"

"No, sir," the sergeant replied. "I can't rightly say as I do."

"You'd have had to serve aboard one of Her Majesty's ships to truly learn to detest this tattoo," Cauling said. "This is the mark of the Moon Shadows, one of the pirate clans that wreaked bloody hell along the coastal trade. Took down a goodly number of British ships, they did." He studied Tsun-Chung closely. "And unless I miss my guess, this is one of the Zhao clan. One of the fiercest of the lot."

Panic welled within Mushu. He struggled against the stranger's grip.

"Not now, boy," the stranger whispered. "Today is their day. Tomorrow is ours."

"I'm sure there are still rewards for this man's head," Cauling announced officiously. He turned to walk away, then spun quickly, plucking a pistol from his coat and leveling the weapon in one smooth motion. "And I'll be collecting them." The pistol barked and the sharp report carried over the flat water of the Whangpu River.

Mushu watched in horror as his father's head snapped back. The British soldiers released Tsun-Chung, and his corpse sprawled over the ragged, scarred wood of the dock. Blood pooled in the ruin of Tsun-Chung's face.

A scream ripped free of Mushu's throat, but it never got past the hard, callused hand that clamped over his mouth. The stranger gripped him more tightly, controlling him and pulling him back.

"Search these men," Cauling ordered. "I'll wager that you find more pirates among them. Any man bearing a mark like this is worth British pounds sterling. As much dead as he may be alive."

The British soldiers spread out at once. They blew their whistles, summoning more forces. Dockworkers scattered before them, obviously afraid that the Britons were going to start killing indiscriminately.

"Boy," the stranger whispered in Mushu's ear.

Mushu continued to struggle, trying desperately to get away. But the man held him tightly, and he could do nothing to free himself.

The stranger yanked harder. "Boy, listen to me if you want to live."

Mushu didn't care if he lived or not. His father had moved them to Shanghai to step away from their outlaw past. Tsun-Chung had wanted to raise his son free of the criminal life he'd known as a pirate. The tattoo Tsun-Chung had worn on his forearm had been with him all his life, just as the one Mushu wore on his chest had been placed on him when he was a boy. The mark had bound them all to the pirates, and put them in fear of their lives from ever leaving.

"Your father," the stranger whispered. "Your father would want you to live. And he would want you to have your revenge. Do you want it?"

Mushu stopped struggling as the British soldiers scattered across the dock. He nodded. Then, when the stranger released his mouth, he said, "Yes."

"Then come with me," the stranger said. "We'll need to get your family, for the Britons will hunt them down. I'll take you from here, to where my friends are. You'll have your revenge against these foreign devils then."

Mushu's eyes burned, but he kept the tears of his raging grief from his cheeks. His father had been wrong. The Moon Shadows were still cursed by Chi-Kan's decision to become a pirate all those years ago. There was no escape; there were only more enemies, more blood to be shed.

1

Hong Kong

"He is an American CIA agent, Miss Zhao. You know that he will lie to you."

Standing in the shadow-filled boathouse near Victoria Harbour in Hong Kong, Saengkeo Zhao studied Johnny Kwan. Kwan was in his midthirties, a year older than she was, a year younger than Syn-Tek, her brother, had been when he had been murdered seven days ago.

"Of course he will lie to me," Saengkeo said. "What remains to be seen is how big the lies will be, and what they will be about."

Kwan gazed back at her, but she couldn't tell what he was thinking. Kwan had always been that way, even when he had been growing up in the Zhao home—always taciturn, always direct. He wore a black suit, favoring dark clothing as he usually did, and black-lensed wraparound sunglasses. He was the warlord for the Moon Shadow triad, the crime family that Saengkeo now ruled.

"Whatever he lies to you about," Kwan said in a calm, still voice, "it will only be about things that will get you killed."

Saengkeo knew that was the truth. Although the CIA and the Moon Shadow triad were supposedly working together—each group for its own benefit—she knew that Rance Stoddard and his agents would walk away from her if they ran risks greater than they were willing to accept.

Looking at the boat, Saengkeo remembered her brother's corpse. Bullets had torn through Syn-Tek's flesh, as well.

"Others have lied to us," Saengkeo reminded him.

"Your brother never lied to either of us," Kwan said defensively.

Saengkeo pinned Kwan with her gaze. "Did you know about this boat?"

Kwan's hesitation was almost imperceptible. "No."

"Syn-Tek kept this from us." Saengkeo knew Kwan couldn't argue with that. He had seen the paperwork that Stoddard had provided that dealt with the true ownership of the cigarette boat. Syn-Tek had purchased the boat, and he had hidden that fact from her.

She had no idea why, but from Stoddard's calm demeanor, she felt certain that the CIA agent had.

From the time that her brother had been killed—Syn-Tek was murdered, she told herself—her life had been chaos. Other triads, sensing weakness on the part of the Moon Shadows, had tried to encroach on their territory. She had dealt with all of them. Only hours ago, at a large meeting of triad leaders, Saengkeo had held one of the triad leaders at knifepoint and threatened him.

It felt, Saengkeo thought, as if the world were falling apart around her. And she had no idea what to do about it except work her way through the lies and half-truths—even when they were ones left by her brother.

Saengkeo wore black jeans, a black turtleneck and a black

leather duster that covered the double shoulder holster containing her Walther Model P-990 QPQ pistols. A black watch cap kept her shoulder-length black hair pulled back from her eyes.

Rance Stoddard stood nearby, engrossed in a conversation over his cell phone, which he kept tucked into his face. He was six feet four inches tall. His thick auburn hair was cut short in a military style. He wore an expensive navy suit.

"Miss Zhao," a voice called over the transceiver Saengkeo wore in her ear.

"What?" Saengkeo asked.

"We have just received news that the Soaring Dragons were attacked in Arizona."

Surprise filled Saengkeo, but she worked hard to keep the emotion from her face. She knew Kwan was privy to the same information. According to information she had gotten at gunpoint from Wai-Lim Yang, the head of the Black Swan triad, the Soaring Dragons had custody of Pei-Ling Bao, a childhood friend of Saengkeo's.

Pei-Ling was a prostitute these days, following in the footsteps of her mother before her. Also, Pei-Ling had gone missing the day after Syn-Tek's murder. Saengkeo didn't believe in coincidences. Until she heard from her friend's lips that she knew nothing of her brother's death, Saengkeo chose to believe that the death of her brother and the disappearance of her friend were somehow connected.

"What of Pei-Ling?" Saengkeo asked.

"I don't know."

"Who did this?"

"The reports are very confusing," the man said. "Some say that the attack was staged by the Border Patrol or the Immigration and Naturalization Service, but others say that one man attacked the convoy and killed all the Soaring Dragons involved in the transportation of the illegal aliens."

"Where did the Soaring Dragons come from before they were in Arizona?"

"Mexico," the man answered. "The Soaring Dragons operate an illegal-alien run out of Mexico, and they buy women to work in the brothels they manage."

One man? The thought whirled through Saengkeo's mind. Who could the one man be, and what could he want?

"What do you want me to do, Miss Zhao?" the man asked.

"Get our attorneys over there," Saengkeo replied. "As soon as they have information about Pei-Ling, I want that information."

"Of course."

Kwan shook his head slightly. His dislike, so much like Syn-Tek's, for Pei-Ling was strong.

At that moment, Stoddard closed his cell phone, glanced at her, then crossed over to Saengkeo.

"You said," Saengkeo stated slowly, "that you were going to explain this cigarette boat and how it came to be in my brother's possession."

The CIA section chief nodded. "You've heard of the Soviet submarine *Kursk*?" Stoddard asked.

"Yes," Saengkeo answered.

"The Russian *mafiya* stole three nuclear payloads from the missiles recovered from the wreckage of the submarine," Stoddard continued. "They had a deal arranged with a Middle Eastern terrorist group. Which group in particular isn't important at the moment. What is important is the fact that your brother agreed to intercept those warheads and turn them over to the United States government. Meaning me."

"Why would Syn-Tek do that?" Saengkeo asked.

"Because I asked him to," Stoddard replied flatly.

Saengkeo looked at the CIA agent, barely resisting the impulse to call Stoddard a liar.

"My agency became aware of the presence of the shipment

too late to scramble an operation into the area," Stoddard continued. "I offered the assignment to Syn-Tek."

Saengkeo glanced at Johnny Kwan standing beside her. Kwan appeared focused on something else entirely, but she knew he tracked every word.

"There was no reason for my brother to take such a risk," Saengkeo said. "The deal my family arranged with you and your agency and government was already in place."

Stoddard shook his head. "Miss Zhao, I know that your brother made you aware of all the circumstances and ramifications of what we were doing."

Saengkeo steeled herself, shoving aside the warring emotions trapped inside her, focusing her thoughts. "You agreed on behalf of your government to help my family get out of Hong Kong, out of the triads and the criminal syndicates where they have been trapped for almost two hundred years." As she spoke, she realized the words belonged to her father, and that mission had been handed down from her great-grandfather Jik-Chang Zhao.

"And in return, you would get closer to the triad families like the Big Circle Society and United Bamboo to feed us more information about their operations."

"I have done that, as did my brother before me, and still you and your agency move so slowly."

Stoddard nodded. "Do you realize the trust that you're asking me—asking my country—to have in you?"

"My father started bargaining with the United States back in the 1970s," Saengkeo replied, raising her voice over the agent's words. "The Moon Shadows were used then—*used,* Agent Stoddard—as spies, and we lost far more than we gained. Members of our family were killed by the Chinese government because of the information they helped your government get. They were all friends and relatives of my father. The immediate families of those caught doing spy work for the United States government were put to death, as well."

"I know that."

The anger surged within Saengkeo, dark and terrible, and wouldn't be denied. She stepped toward Stoddard. Beside her, Kwan barely flinched, as if he considered stopping her or was thinking of protecting her, but he didn't move any further.

"I knew some of those families," Saengkeo said. "I knew the husbands and wives and children. They were murdered in cold blood for the risks they took for your government."

"What they did," Stoddard said quietly, "made a difference."

"No difference to my family. Twenty years have passed, and my family was not given the aid we were promised."

"You're getting the aid now. Those sacrifices and that twenty years have made a difference. You're slowly getting your family out of Hong Kong, into legitimate businesses in the United States and Canada, and other U.S.-friendly countries. What we promised your father, what we promised your family, all of that is coming true."

"My brother is dead because we have been waiting."

"My government needed to believe in you," Stoddard replied. "During the past twenty years, my agency and other agencies have seen that the Moon Shadows have continued to try to ease out of illegitimate businesses here and around the world."

"We've been getting out of illegal businesses since the 1920s," Saengkeo pointed out. "If anyone needed to see a trend, they could have found one then."

"Our records regarding triad organizations aren't that complete," Stoddard argued. "China was a mess after the Boxer Rebellion, then Japan invaded before World War II. Once that was done, they allied themselves with Russia and set up a closed-door policy that wasn't opened again until the 1970s under the Nixon administration. Even then, our resources were deployed primarily to watching government actions, not those of criminals."

Saengkeo barely restrained herself from speaking. She breathed through her nose, forcing herself to relax.

"Until your father offered his services," Stoddard went on, "no one in my government would have been willing to help you. Those losses incurred twenty years ago built the foundation for the agreement that we have reached."

"And yet," Saengkeo argued, "if the new Chinese government taking the place of the old men that have run this country for so long had not linked themselves so much to the crime syndicates in these past few years, perhaps that agreement would never have been honored."

"I don't know, Miss Zhao," Stoddard answered. "I can't change history. What happened then was then. This is now. And you've seen my interest in you and your family."

"Self-serving, is it not?" Kwan stated matter-of-factly.

"Everything is about business these days," Stoddard said, ignoring Kwan's accusation. "Espionage is about business, and politics is about business. Today, it isn't about how much land you control. It's about how much of the market you control. Organized crime has known that forever, and the Chinese government is opening itself up more and more to involvement with the triad families because of their international reach. The triads know more about how to penetrate markets and compete economically with the rest of the world. China wants to grow."

"And that scares your country," Saengkeo said.

"Hell yes," Stoddard said. "That's why there's so much controversy over what to do with Taiwan. Whether to watch the Chinese government annex the country, or whether to try to help Taiwan become an independent country."

"A puppet country of the United States, you mean," Saengkeo said. "A willing American military base ready to strike against China."

Stoddard shook his head. "You want to move your people into the Western world, Miss Zhao. Don't be so quick to put my country down."

Saengkeo turned from the CIA agent and wrapped her arms around herself. Her hands and knees trembled. The whole day seemed to be catching up with her. The battle aboard *Goldfish*, the showdown with Yang and knowing there would be repercussions from him at some point, the incident at the triad meeting all came home at once.

She stared at the bullet-riddled cigarette boat, feeling the emptiness of the craft echo within her. Despite everything else going on in her life, the answer to the most crucial question on her heart was here. "What happened to my brother?"

Stoddard waited a moment, as if assembling his thoughts. "Syn-Tek agreed to go after the nuclear weapons the Russian *mafiya* had for sale."

"At your insistence."

"If you choose to view the matter that way, I can't stop you."

"And Syn-Tek—" a lump swelled to painful proportions within Saengkeo's throat "—never told me of this because you ordered him not to."

"I didn't tell your brother anything like that," Stoddard replied. "I knew Syn-Tek well. I knew I couldn't order something like that. At first, when you didn't come to me after his death, I didn't know what to expect. He didn't tell you because he wanted you kept safe from harm."

Saengkeo remembered the days of silence that had ensued after Syn-Tek's body had been discovered. At the time, she hadn't noticed them because she had been swallowed up in her grief. Later, those days had become suspicious, causing the uneasiness that continued between herself and the CIA agent.

"When I figured out that you hadn't known about Syn-Tek's mission," Stoddard said, "I didn't know how to tell you."

"So you waited until today and gave me the picture of this boat."

"Yes."

"Why?"

"Because of Yang this morning," Stoddard replied.

Saengkeo turned to face the American. "As revenge for using you and your people as I did?" Her anger almost escaped her.

"No," Stoddard reassured her. "Because it wasn't until then that I realized what you were doing. You were looking for your brother's killer, thinking you were going to find that person among the rival triad families." He shrugged. "You're not going to find Syn-Tek's killers there, Miss Zhao. No one among the triads killed him."

"His body—was found on the docks."

"I left it there," Stoddard said.

Saengkeo stepped forward, but Kwan moved smoothly between her and the CIA agent. Before Saengkeo knew it, the Walther was in her hand again, coming up.

Kwan caught her hand and restrained her. "No," he said.

Saengkeo stared into the merciless depths of Kwan's sunglasses. "This bastard left Syn-Tek's body on the docks," she whispered hoarsely. Her throat felt constricted, too tight.

Kwan spoke in English, never taking his eyes from Saengkeo's. "Where was Syn-Tek killed?"

"At sea," Stoddard answered. "Some of the people who came to clean up afterward wanted to drop the body into the ocean. I refused, and I took full responsibility for bringing the body back. I had to pull rank to see that done."

Saengkeo surged against Kwan, then forced herself to relax. She stared at Stoddard.

"I couldn't just abandon Syn-Tek there," the CIA agent said. "His body needed to be honored. Your need to know and to grieve, Miss Zhao, needed to be honored."

For a long moment, Saengkeo stood there, then the anger melted from her, leaving her shaken and empty. "What of the other men with my brother?" There was talk of the men that had gone missing at the same time Syn-Tek's body was discovered. No one knew what had happened to them, only that they had last been seen with Syn-Tek.

"They all died."

"I'll want the names of the dead," Saengkeo said. "Their families need to be told."

"Of course."

Saengkeo stared into Kwan's dark gaze. "You didn't know?" she asked.

"No," Kwan replied solemnly. "Not until this minute." Slowly he released her and stepped away. "Forgive me for daring so greatly."

"There's nothing to forgive. You have always been my brother." Saengkeo holstered the Walther, and she knew Stoddard was watching her every move. "Who killed Syn-Tek?"

"The Russians."

"Syn-Tek failed to get the weapons back?" Somehow the thought that her brother had lost his life in a failed mission seemed even worse.

"Your brother," Stoddard said, "was a hero. He stopped the Russians and retrieved the nuclear weapon that was aboard the ship."

"*Weapon?*" Saengkeo looked at Stoddard. "I thought you said there were three weapons."

"There were supposed to be three," Stoddard agreed. "When Syn-Tek got on board, there was only one. He took that one and sunk the warhead at a prescribed point where a U.S. Navy sub was later able to perform a recovery."

"Then my brother was still alive."

"At the time, yes. Before he could reach Hong Kong again, another Russian ship overtook him." Stoddard glanced at the damaged cigarette boat. "His own vessel was barely navigable. They boarded the cigarette boat and killed your brother and his crew."

Saengkeo's eyes burned at the thought of her brother being shot down so ruthlessly, but she held back her tears. After the way she had grieved, she was surprised that she had any left.

"How did the boat get here?" she asked when she could speak again.

"I had the boat towed here at night," Stoddard answered. "When you put a tarp over the boat, no one can see the damage in the darkness. The retrieval crew that got the nuclear weapon also patched the boat up enough to keep from sinking."

"Why?"

"I didn't feel like I had a choice. I didn't know how Syn-Tek had structured the deal regarding the vessel. I didn't want to leave a trail that led back to the Moon Shadows family if the boat suddenly disappeared or was found in the vicinity of the attack on the Russian ship. We could have sunk it, but I couldn't take the chance that it might wash up on shore and lead someone to Syn-Tek." He paused. "Or to your family."

"The Americans have possession of the weapon my brother intercepted?"

"Yes." Stoddard took a deep breath. "That's one of the most highly classified secrets my country is keeping these days. I've risked a lot by telling you that."

Saengkeo didn't know whether to believe Stoddard or not. Even though she didn't know much about the man, she'd seen enough to know that he didn't release any information without hoping to buy something back. There was another shoe somewhere here that hadn't yet dropped.

"You're holding something back," Saengkeo said.

Stoddard hesitated only a moment. "We think we've found another of the warheads."

For a moment, silence hung heavily in the room.

Saengkeo waited, knowing what Stoddard had come there to ask and refusing to make it any easier for the CIA agent.

"This is an indelicate position for the United States to be in," Stoddard went on. "If we knew for certain that the ship we suspect has the warhead on board, we could go after it."

"But you don't know for certain," Saengkeo said.

"No." Stoddard looked uncomfortable for a moment. "On behalf of the United States government, pursuant to the agreement that government has already entered into with your family, we're asking for help in this matter."

"You want me to get the warhead for you."

After a brief pause, Stoddard said, "Yes."

"The United States would have deniability in the matter. The word of a known criminal family against the word of the most powerful nation in the world."

Stoddard didn't bother to deny the charges.

"And what would my family get out of such an undertaking?" Saengkeo demanded.

"Further recognition that your family wants out of the criminal life it has been involved with for the past two hundred years," Stoddard said.

"When will they start to believe?"

"They already have, Miss Zhao."

"Do you understand what you're asking? That I infiltrate the Big Circle Society and United Bamboo organizations, and still manage to steal nuclear weapons the United States government can't get on its own?"

"It's not that the United States can't recover the warhead," Stoddard said. "It's just that the information we have is...unreliable. All that my government is asking is that you send in a team to verify the report."

"By invading the ship?"

"If necessary."

Saengkeo turned away from Stoddard, her eyes running along the bullet-riddled hull of the cigarette boat. She felt trapped, and at the same time part of her didn't care. Nothing was as it should have been. Not enough of her people were being moved to safety, and without a mass exodus at some point, many of them wouldn't be saved.

"Miss Zhao," Stoddard prompted, "I need an answer to give to my people. Otherwise, they'll choose an alternative means."

"An alternative means won't risk my family any further."

"But you will lose some credibility."

Saengkeo whirled on the CIA agent. "When we agreed to infiltrate the triads for the American government, no mention was made of recovering nuclear bombs."

"They're not bombs," Stoddard said. "In fact, those devices can't even be detonated without the proper codes. Those have already been delivered to the terrorist buyers, but until they get the warheads, those codes won't do any good."

"Whether there is the danger of a nuclear explosion or not, there still remains a danger to the interception team you're asking me to send in."

Stoddard regarded her with a flat gaze. "I'm also offering a chance to strike back at the *mafiya* organization that killed Syn-Tek."

"I'm trying to take care of my family," Saengkeo said. "As my brother did. As my father did, and my father before him. Avenging my dead brother won't help my family."

"Doing this thing," Stoddard said, "will go a long way toward—"

"We're through talking, Agent Stoddard."

Anger showed on Stoddard's face for a moment. He started to say something further, but Kwan took him by the arm and escorted the CIA agent toward the door.

"You have until morning to give me your answer," Stoddard called over his shoulder. "After that, I can't help you."

Saengkeo didn't respond. There was too much for her to get control of, too many different paths she could follow. She stared at the cigarette boat, wishing she knew which course was best, wishing that Syn-Tek were still there. But he wasn't. And in the end, even he had held his secrets, gambling with his life for the betterment of their family.

How could she do any less? And yet, how could she throw her life away unwisely?

2

Arizona

"How many times do I have to tell you that I don't know why those men were holding me?"

Mack Bolan stood at the patio doors of the motel and peered out at the neon-colored night over Scottsdale. After quitting the battlezone on Interstate 8, the soldier had made his way to the city through back roads and avoided the roadblocks established by the Arizona State Police and the Border Patrol. According to the live-breaking news televised on the set in the corner, no one knew who had slain the Chinese traffickers, but there were definite suspects being sought.

The woman Bolan had saved from the traffickers' Winnebago sat on the couch with her legs curled under her. So far, she hadn't even offered her name. She was pretty—he had to give her that—and she moved like a cat, muscles sliding under tawny skin with an eroticism that was definitely engineered. She wore one of the motel-room robes, wrapped around her and barely keeping her modesty intact. Not that Bolan believed for an instant that the woman was modest. Her moves and the way she tried to take control of the situation were professional.

"Have you been in the United States before?" Bolan asked.

"A few times." Her English was almost uninflected but carried a British accent.

"What brought you here?"

"Business."

"Whose?" Bolan asked.

"Sometimes mine. Sometimes a friend's."

"What friend?"

She shook her head.

"Maybe you'd like to answer these questions for an INS agent."

She shrugged. "The INS will ask me questions about what I'm doing here. I'll tell them I was kidnapped." Pushing her hands out, she revealed the heavy bruising and scab-covered sores on her wrists, as well as a healthy amount of cleavage. "I'm betting they'll believe me." She smiled indolently. "I think you'd hate the idea of me being questioned by the immigration service more than I would."

"Maybe I could reunite you with the snakeheads."

She regarded him for a long, cool moment. "You're not the type, Mr. Strong and Silent Guy."

The tack was frustrating, but Bolan knew he didn't have anything else to go on. Holding on to the woman for long wasn't an ideal situation, though. He didn't trust her, and doing without sleep for much longer was going to be hard, as well as harmful.

"Why did you come looking for me?" she asked him.

Bolan shook his head.

The woman smiled again. "Since neither of us is getting the information we want from the other, maybe we could find something else to do." Her meaning was suggestive and unmistakable.

Bolan didn't answer.

Without another word, the woman uncoiled from the couch and approached him. She stood a head shorter than him, but he could feel the heat coming from the womanly curves beneath the white terry-cloth robe. As she smiled up at him, leaning in as if to kiss him, one of her hands ran lightly across his crotch, but hard enough to get his attention. The move was also designed to distract him from the fact that she was trying to get to his wallet.

The Executioner caught both the woman's hands and avoided her attempted kiss. "No," Bolan said.

Sour suspicion colored the woman's face as she stepped back and pulled her hands free. "So now I'm not good enough for you?"

"That's not it."

"Oh," she said, exasperated. "You're all about the mission. Is that it?"

"Something like that," Bolan answered.

"Well, let me clue you in, Mr. Nice Guys Wear Black. Boy Scouts don't leave bodies scattered all over an American interstate without talking to the authorities."

"You were unconscious," Bolan said. "You don't know who I talked to."

"If you'd talked to the authorities," she told him, "I'd be locked up now instead of hiding out in a motel room with you."

"You've had experience?"

The smile reappeared, chasing away the sour look. "Let's just say that I've learned to appreciate handcuffs." She turned and walked away. "I'm bored and I'm tired. The shower I had when we first got here didn't do much more than knock the road grit off me." She glanced over her shoulder, stripping out of the terry-cloth robe in front of the bathroom door. The robe pooled at her feet.

"If you want to continue your inquisition, it's definitely going to be on more intimate terms."

She walked into the bathroom, rolling her naked hips enticingly.

The sight, Bolan realized, wasn't an entirely unwelcome one. He watched as she prepared her bath, his mind not occupied with the woman's lush figure but with the puzzle she presented.

Steam filled the bathroom as the woman lounged on the side of the big tub. She waved to him. "Come on. There's a big tub. It even comes with water jets. I could show you a really good time."

Bolan grinned at her, amused in spite of the frustration she caused him. His cell phone rang. He pulled the phone from his pocket, then crossed the room and closed the door to the bathroom. There was no question that the conversation about to take place wasn't for the woman's ears. The bathroom was enclosed and there wasn't enough crawl space in the ceiling to allow escape. Unless the woman figured out how to slip down through the drain, she wasn't going anywhere.

"Can we talk?" Barbara Price asked.

"Yeah," Bolan said.

"We found her," the Stony Man mission controller said. "Her name is Pei-Ling Bao. Her last known place of residence, listed on her international visa—which is current, by the way—is Hong Kong."

"But she arrived here without her visa," Bolan said, "and without passing through customs."

"Bingo."

Bolan gazed at the notebook computer and miniature scanner lying on the motel desk. He'd used graphite from a gun-cleaning kit to take the woman's fingerprints, transferred them to plastic tape, scanned them into the computer and put the images up on the FTP site he was currently using to liaise with Stony Man Farm. He'd also used the digital camera to take her picture and send that along.

"What's her story?" the warrior asked.

"She's a high-paid prostitute," Price said. "Primarily, she works out of Hong Kong. Lives on the island. According to Interpol records, she's worked the cruise ships around the South China Sea, the Caribbean and the Mediterranean."

"Busy," Bolan commented. And that explained her ease with her current situation.

"Bao's also been deported as an undesirable alien from England, Paris and twice from the United States."

"All for prostitution?"

"Yes."

Bolan turned the information over in his head. "Make the tie to the snakeheads."

"I can't. They belonged to the Soaring Dragons, a relatively small Chinese wanna-be gang that specializes in hard-core crime. Trafficking in people, as well as drugs. They keep up the payments necessary to traffic immigrants by muling cocaine up from Colombia."

"If the woman is from Hong Kong," Bolan pointed out, "the Soaring Dragons have got to be connected with someone there."

"I'm checking into it, but the possibilities are just exploding. The Soaring Dragons have done work for anyone that would pay them. They're basically common property for the triads."

"Maybe the state police here or the INS can turn up something."

"Striker, at this point no one was found alive at that site. Whatever few survivors there were after that firefight evaporated before the law-enforcement teams arrived."

Bolan considered his options. "Maybe a trip down to Mexico is in order. Rattle a few cages down that way and see what I can turn up on the Soaring Dragons."

"Perhaps," Price said. "But Leo turned up something in New York that you might be interested in."

Bolan wasn't surprised. Leo Turrin wasn't a guy to walk away from a game still on the table.

"Leo parlayed the local don's goodwill toward a certain Black Ace, along with a healthy dose of paranoia," Price said, "into an intensive dig into the Russian *mafiya*'s business. The don's people found a whisper about one of the packages that went missing."

"I thought there was only one package." A chill raced through Bolan.

"So did I," Price replied, "until I caught a rumor that a Navy sub recovered one of the packages below the area of the pirate attack."

"No confirmation?"

"None. Even Hal can't get a weather forecast on the situation. The Navy is playing this one close to the vest, and my guess is those orders come straight out of the White House."

"Dropping one package," Bolan said, "leaves two. Together or separate?"

"We have no way of knowing," Price said. "Hopefully, the remaining two are all in one basket."

"Where's the basket?" Bolan asked.

"On a Russian cargo ship in the Indian Ocean. The ship passed through Singapore and through the Java Sea only hours ago."

"How certain are you about the intel?"

"I'm not. This could turn out to be a milk run. But this is our angle, Striker, one that we've earned ourselves. If I were surer of the information, we'd probably be required to turn everything we have over to the White House and let the

Agency teams deal with it. I've got Jack en route to you, but whether you make the hop is your call."

Jack Grimaldi was the chief flying ace for the Stony Man Farm operation. He was also one of Bolan's closest and oldest friends. The Executioner had waded through the Mafia trenches playing cat-and-mouse with Leo Turrin, but Jack Grimaldi had been there for some of the bloodiest battles.

"We'll play it," Bolan said, glancing at the closed bathroom door. "I've about run out of options here. And that part of the world seems to be where the action is."

"What are you going to do with the woman?"

"At this point she's not much use to the mission. I was going to turn her over to the INS."

"I was going to suggest that," Price said. "She has a tattoo on her upper right shoulder. You noticed it yet?"

"Yeah."

"It's a triad symbol representing a family called the Moon Shadows. That's why the face is obscured the way it is. The Moon Shadows are an old triad, going back two hundred years. I'll work up a dossier on them, too."

"Something caught your eye?" Bolan asked.

"The head of the Moon Shadows," Price said, "was a guy named Syn-Tek Zhao. Less than a day after the attack on *Jadviga,* he turned up dead. Nobody knows how he got that way."

"Maybe that's a little too convenient," Bolan said.

"That's what I was thinking. Jack will be there in a few hours. I'll set up a safehouse to hold Pei-Ling Bao for a few days. Until we figure out whether she knows anything worth knowing."

Hong Kong

SITTING IN THE QUIET darkness gathered in the play area of the Moon Shadow building, Saengkeo Zhao tried to recapture the sound of the children laughing and playing earlier that day. With everything that had happened, remembering that she'd been there and heard the children less than eighteen hours ago seemed almost impossible—like some warped and macabre joke.

Her whole life seemed to have changed in just those few hours. Only, while living through them, the time hadn't seemed so short. Living moment by moment all day long hadn't allowed for the compression of time.

She held her cell phone in her hands. Rance Stoddard's number was burned into her brain.

But she hadn't called yet.

As she sat in solitude, trying to choose the correct path, her phone rang.

"Yes."

"I have news about Pei-Ling Bao," Johnny Kwan announced.

Saengkeo listened to the story Kwan told her about Pei-Ling's kidnapping from the Soaring Dragons in Arizona. A few of the triad members had escaped the wrath of the lone vigilante and lived to tell the tale. Some of the people Kwan worked with in the States relayed the stories.

"This man wasn't a law-enforcement person?" Saengkeo asked when Kwan had finished his detailed report.

"A policeman would have waited for other policemen," Kwan pointed out. "If Pei-Ling were taken into custody, my contacts would have found that out, as well. They have sources. Whoever this man is, he's not working with the police."

"What about with the American intelligence agencies?"

"They don't work alone. This man did. He's something different."

Saengkeo's heart hardened. "Not different," she said. "If Pei-Ling has been harmed, that man is dead. Just like the man that gave Pei-Ling to the Soaring Dragons."

Kwan was silent.

Staring out over the city, able to see the dark water stirring in Victoria Harbour between the lighted ships, Saengkeo said, "Get the teams ready for the mission."

"You are accepting Stoddard's terms, then?"

"There was never a real choice," Saengkeo said. "Stoddard knew that when he offered us the mission. Maybe he didn't have a choice, either. A wise man once said that in order to properly fish, you first have to cast bread out onto the water. Tomorrow night, we're going fishing. One way or another, we'll know soon whether our trust has been well invested or betrayed."

Above the Indian Ocean

"SAENGKEO ZHAO IS the acting head of the Moon Shadow triad."

Seated in the copilot's seat of the Grumman HU-16B Albatross amphibious plane, Bolan listened to Barbara Price spin out the story over the aircraft's radio. The Albatross came equipped with a nonstandard satellite receiver that allowed the use of advanced communications. He even had access to the Internet, and that had allowed him to download the encrypted files from Stony Man Farm.

Although he'd slept some during the jet flight out of Scottsdale, Arizona, Bolan still felt worn and ragged. With Jack Grimaldi manning the private Learjet, they'd made the jump to L.A., then to Hawaii and the Philippines, crossing the international dateline out over the Pacific Ocean. They'd made the journey in a little less than thirteen hours. With the time differential and the speed of the Lear, they'd left Los Angeles at 4:47 a.m. on Thursday and arrived in the Philippines shortly before 11:00 a.m. on Friday, local time.

Grimaldi had spent time arranging for the amphibious plane and the Tekna Diver Propulsion Vehicle. The DPV was packed in the cargo space. Bolan intended to use the DPV on the final approach to the cargo ship. The plane had also been modified with extra fuel tanks, bumping the near three-thousand-mile cruising range up another thousand miles. After refueling in Singapore, they were well within striking distance of the Russian cargo ship sailing through the southernmost fringes of the Bay of Bengal in the Indian Ocean.

The cargo ship stayed out in international waters but was tracking the coastline. Her manifest claimed *Charity's Smile* to be bound for Egypt for trade, but Bolan and Price agreed that the ship was probably set up to deliver the packages the vessel carried somewhere along the way.

Since Turrin's relayed information had reached Stony Man, Kurtzman and his cybernetic spies had kept the ship under observation. No other ships had made contact with *Charity's Smile* since she'd left Singapore. As long as the ship hadn't off-loaded in Singapore, she presumably still carried one or both of the missing nuclear weapons.

While in the Philippines, Bolan had seen to his own gear. Taking the weapons out of Scottsdale hadn't been an option. However, the Philippines was still a hotbed of black market activity.

The soldier was rigged out in a formfitting black wet suit. A combat harness and weapons filled a waterproof bag back with the battery-powered DPV in the cargo area.

"Saengkeo Zhao is related to Syn-Tek Zhao?" he asked.

"They were brother and sister."

Bolan rubbed at the stubble on his chin. "A woman heading up a triad crime family is unusual."

"She," Price said with a note of respect, "is an unusual woman. She's in her early thirties, but she has a Master's in business management from the States."

Bolan regarded the woman on the notebook computer's screen. He tapped the mousepad and flipped through the pictures Price had included in the digital information packet she'd sent. During the past hour, he'd skimmed the details of Saengkeo Zhao's life. She was an incredible woman.

"Despite the education," Price went on, "if she is involved in the present bit of business, you're dealing with an efficient killer. She's been trained in a half-dozen martial arts, handguns and military armament. No database I've accessed so far has recorded an accurate number of confirmed kills. Ask a different agency, you get a different number."

"All family business?" Bolan asked.

"Most of it. Rival gangs that tried to kill her or someone close to her."

"Any kills outside the crime syndicates?"

"Maybe. There are unconfirmed rumors. The latest news I have is that Saengkeo Zhao and the Moon Shadow family were responsible for the destruction of a mini-cruise ship in Victoria Harbour about twenty-four hours ago."

"She's got a lot of irons in the fire," Bolan commented. "But that doesn't mean she's involved with this."

"Agreed," Price said. "I've always found it better to know too much about a situation than to know too little. With the situation shaping up in China between the government agencies and the triads, we may be doing business with Saengkeo Zhao at some point. For now, I think it's enough that Pei-Ling Bao ties in with the Moon Shadow organization to warrant a closer look. Any closer look we take is going to include Saengkeo Zhao."

Bolan tapped the mousepad more, going back through the pictures. He stopped on the picture of a young man with a hard face. There were several shots of him, as well. "What about Johnny Kwan?"

"At present," Price said, "Kwan is Saengkeo Zhao's right-hand man. He's a cipher. Nobody seems to know where he came from, but he showed up in the Zhao household one day.

He's vicious and cold-blooded. Saengkeo's father did everything but adopt Kwan into the family."

Bolan scanned the documents, opening the folder Price had set up to hold personal information on everyone she'd deemed necessary to know about. "Kwan served as Syn-Tek Zhao's lieutenant, as well."

"Yes."

Sitting back in the copilot's seat, Bolan regarded the man's image frozen on the notebook computer. "Interesting that Kwan wasn't with Syn-Tek when Syn-Tek was murdered."

"I thought so, too."

"Saengkeo Zhao may have more problems than she bargained for."

"Pei-Ling Bao is a close friend of Saengkeo Zhao's," Price stated. "The Bao woman's kidnapping was done for a reason."

"Ransom?"

"That's the first thing that comes to mind, but none of the intelligence community seemed to know that the Bao woman was missing, much less if there was a ransom demand for her. Maybe the overlap between the nuclear arms, Syn-Tek's murder and Pei-Ling's kidnapping are consequences that overlap."

"I've never been a big believer in consequence," Bolan said.

"Me, neither."

"Hey, Sarge," Grimaldi called from the pilot's seat.

Bolan glanced up at his friend.

Grimaldi was on the wiry side, dressed in a brown bomber jacket with patches, fitting the look of the old amphibian plane. The ace pilot had been proud of the Grumman, reiterating the aircraft's history of military service throughout World War II, Korea, as a search-and-rescue plane used by the U.S. Coast Guard. All of the planes had been mustered out of military service in 1973, but several of them remained active with private owners and companies throughout Asia.

"Coming up on your drop zone," Grimaldi explained. "I'm picking up the GPS ping Aaron's laid down for me."

"How far out are we?"

Grimaldi checked his instruments. "Four miles and closing. If you're ready."

Bolan nodded. Delays meant fuel consumption. The plan was for Grimaldi to stay on hand, serving as a satellite relay for Bolan's tactical communications gear, then a quick means of exfiltration once the job was done.

"Let's do it," the Executioner said. He closed down the computer and took off his headgear. Retreating to the cargo space, the warrior quickly pulled on the scuba tanks, fins and mask, then secured a parachute over all that. Ready, he muscled the DPV to the cargo door in the side of the plane. Sliding the door open, he peered out at the flat, dark sea below as the wind hammered him.

Full dark had fallen over the Indian Ocean almost two hours earlier. Distinguishing the horizon, where the night met the water, was almost impossible.

Scanning the sea ahead of the Grumman amphibian, Bolan made out the Russian cargo ship's running lights. The lights resembled hollow yellow wisps against the flat darkness of the water. He adjusted his mask a final time and activated the radio built inside the headgear.

"Do you read me, Fly-By Knight?" Bolan said.

"Fly-By Knight reads you, Striker."

Bolan caught up his equipment bag in one hand. He attached the bag's strap to his belt, then hooked the strap for the DPV to his ankle.

The Tekna Diver Propulsion Vehicle was nearly three feet long. Powered by a battery-driven fan propeller, the DPV was capable of remaining underwater and pulling a diver. The machine would save Bolan a lot of expended energy and time swimming to an interception course with the cargo ship. Pursuing the cargo ship wasn't an option because the DPV wouldn't be able to keep up.

"Stony Base," Bolan said, "do you read?"

"Stony Base reads you five by five," Price answered.

"Good enough," Bolan replied. "Count the drop down, Fly-By Knight."

"Drop zone coming up," Grimaldi said. "Ten, nine, eight..."

When Grimaldi hit zero, Bolan shoved the DPV through the cargo door, heaved out the weapons bag and leaped after them before either hit the end of their restraining straps. He plummeted from the aircraft, buffeted by the wind and feeling for an instant that he was flying instead of falling.

As close as he was to the sea because of the Grumman's low flight ceiling, Bolan pulled his chute cord as soon as he felt he was clear of the plane. The chute deployed with a familiar hissing pop, but the drag created by the equipment bag and the DPV was considerable.

"You're on target for the interception course, Striker," Price said over the headset.

A few short feet above the water, Bolan cut the parachute harness free and dropped into the water. Both the weapons bag and the DPV were buoyant so neither would drag him under.

Cold ocean water closed over Bolan's head. Instinctively he held his breath, then remembered he was wearing the scuba. He started breathing, then pulled himself to the DPV, started the machine and pulled the equipment bag to him, as well. Adjusting the bag for neutral buoyancy, Bolan pulled the strap over his head, securing the bag around his chest. He took up the DPV's motorcycle handgrips, attached the slim cable from the DPV to his weight belt and started toward the approaching Russian cargo ship.

3

Bolan twisted the handlebars on the Tekna DPV and angled toward the surface. He'd been in the ocean for seventeen minutes according to the dive watch he wore under long gloves. He glanced to the east when he surfaced and saw the dark bulk of the cargo ship closing in.

"Stony Base, this is Striker. Do you copy?" Bolan said.

"Stony Base copies," Price called back over the radio frequency they'd set up.

"Fly-By Knight copies," Grimaldi chimed in.

Bolan looked up into the dark heavens but couldn't see Grimaldi's Albatross anywhere. The pilot would be running with his lights off, working by instrumentation. There wasn't even an echo of the propellers that could be heard over the silence of the sea.

"Your target is 470 yards and closing, Striker," Price warned. "With the speed she has up, making the snag could be difficult."

"Understood, Stony Base." Bolan rummaged in his weapons bag and brought out the CO_2-powered grappling launcher. After affixing the padded grappling hook, he steered the DPV across the ocean, drawing within twenty yards of where the cargo ship would pass.

Shouldering the launcher, resting an elbow on the DPV, Bolan fired at the cargo ship's railing. The hook flared through the night sky, trailing line out behind, then dropped onto the ship's deck. From the way the line jittered and bounced, Bolan knew he didn't have the purchase he needed. If the hook didn't catch, Grimaldi would have to pick him up and they'd have to try again.

The line jerked taut with a sudden snap, almost catching him off guard. He paid out more line from the launcher while he hooked the weapons bag over one shoulder. The line was kernmantle dynamic rope, the choice of mountain climbers who needed the elasticity built into the rope. Pulled by the cargo ship, Bolan hydroplaned across the sea, taking a beating for a time until he climbed the rope through the water and was able to brace his feet against the ship's hull and start up.

"Target acquired," Bolan growled over the radio link. His back and shoulders burned from the effort of the climb. Making a loop in the line that would support his weight, he kicked off his flippers and stood in the loop.

Quickly he slid on a pair of athletic shoes he'd packed in the weapons bag, then shrugged into the combat harness and Kevlar vest. A counterterrorist drop rig along his right thigh held a .44 Magnum Desert Eagle. He carried a silenced SIG-Sauer P-226 in a shoulder holster, and a dive knife already rode his right calf. He clipped on extra magazines for the pistols, as well as for the MP-5 SD3 he carried for his lead weapon, then added a clutch of frag and smoke grenades and a shoulder satchel of C-4 plastic explosives. A miniaturized digital video camera with its own feed on a secondary frequency that Grimaldi hosted was buckled over his heart on the combat harness. He stripped the headgear off, but kept the radio that fit into his ear canal and connected him with Grimaldi and Price.

Dropping the empty bag, the Executioner climbed the rope, reached the deck and peered around. Tarp-covered stacks of crates filled the midships decks. The ship gave every appearance of a merchant craft interested only in finding some kind of meager profit.

With no one in sight, the soldier heaved himself over the side and rolled onto the deck. In a heartbeat, he was crouched beside the cargo hold.

The hold wasn't locked. Bolan lifted the heavy wood-and-metal hatch and looked down.

Light from three lanterns placed around the hold ghosted along the ship's interior, leaving shadows scattered all around. Music echoed inside, overrun by voices of men talking in Russian. Tracking the voices, the Executioner spotted four men playing cards in the stern.

He eased down the steps, grateful that none of the lantern light hit the companionway directly. At the foot of the stairs, he crept through the stacks of crates. Evidently, *Charity's Smile* was making every effort to look like a conventional merchant ship, because there were nonperishable foods, farm equipment and boxes of computer equipment on pallets everywhere.

Bolan stepped out of the shadows with the MP-5 in his hands. "Nobody move," he commanded in Russian.

Two of the men were young, obviously there as hired muscle more than for their sailing abilities. They reached for pistols in shoulder rigs under their pea jackets.

Two tribursts from the silenced machine pistol left the two men sprawled across the deck and blood sprayed across the crates behind them. Shifting his aim to the other two men, Bolan looked meaningfully at them.

Both men raised their hands.

"I came for the cargo," the Executioner said.

One of the men, a grizzled old guy with a stained red watch cap and gray whiskers, looked around. "But there is the cargo. You see it already."

"The *real* cargo," Bolan replied. "The one that they've been hiding."

The old man started to shake his head.

The other man spoke up quickly. "Do you want to die for these men, then, Fyodor? For these criminals?" He spit on the metal deck at their feet. "These men have killed the other crew. Men that you and I shared our lives with. They've kept the captain and us to run the ship for them. When they have finished with us and they make the delivery, do you think they will have any compassion for us?"

The man in the red watch cap shook his head angrily. "No, Ivan, and do you think this man, this man who is so quick to kill these two, is going to spare any compassion for us?"

The second man stood. "If I'm to die, then I will die as Ivan Kirinov, as my own self and not some scared old man as I have lived these past few weeks."

He glanced at Bolan. "You are American, yes?"

"Yeah," Bolan agreed.

"Come. I will show you where they have hidden their precious secret cargo."

Bolan motioned the other man to his feet and into line with Kirinov. The warrior's combat senses remained alert.

"How many men are aboard the ship?" Bolan asked.

"The captain and five more sailors," Kirinov answered. "The damn criminals number eighteen men." Then he nodded back at the corpses around the card table. "Sixteen now, I suppose."

"Do you know who they're working with?"

Kirinov shrugged. "They're criminals. Today they work for one man. Tomorrow they work for another. After that, who knows?"

"What do you know about the cargo?"

"Only that they're very secretive. And that they're supposed to have a buyer that will pick the cargo up before we reach our destination in Egypt."

"How soon before they make delivery?" Bolan took in all the old man's information, adding in the complication of innocent sailors aboard the cargo ship. That had been a consideration in the early stages of his plans; now their presence was confirmed.

Kirinov shrugged. "Some of them play cards with us upon occasion, and share meals with us, but if they know when the trade is to be made, they're not saying." He walked to the stern bulkhead wall. "They made a hiding place for the cargo, and they thought that they were so sly that we didn't see. As if we don't know this ship that some of us have served on so long." He knelt and pressed on the flooring.

A section of the floor came up, revealing dark recesses.

Bolan kept the two men loosely covered with the machine pistol, took a penlight from his combat harness and peered inside. A long crate filled the space on a platform welded to the ship's substructure. "I need the crate opened."

Taking a small crowbar from his coveralls, Kirinov climbed down into the hiding place and opened the crate. Nails shrilled as they were pulled free.

Bolan played the penlight over the gleaming metal inside. He held the light between his teeth and used the digital video camera, sending images back to Price and the Stony Man intelligence teams.

"That's one of the warhead types *Kursk* carried," Price confirmed. "I'll put this through to Hal and let him kick it up to the Man. There are nearby military operations that we might be able to cull Special Forces teams from to make the recovery."

"Do that. I'll put things in play here." Bolan put away the digital camera. He glanced at Kirinov. "Is this the only one?"

The old sailor nodded. He looked uneasy, as if more aware of the machine pistol in Bolan's hand.

The Executioner slung the machine pistol. "If I can, I'm going to take this ship with a team. That's a nuclear warhead."

Kirinov turned to the other sailor. "See, Fyodor? I told you these criminals were messing with very bad things."

The other sailor hung his head as if ashamed.

"I'm going to mine this ship," Bolan said, taking up the pack of C-4 munitions over his shoulder.

Both sailors looked horrified.

"We'll never be able to outrun a nuclear blast," Fyodor said.

"The explosives won't set off the nuke. I'm going to blow out the ship's prow as a last resort. In the meantime, we need to get the crew out of harm's way without alerting the men who hold this ship. Do you have a place you can gather them?"

"Back by the boom arm," Kirinov said. "That area is always oily and messy. They never follow us there. During the times we've been in port, they've kept us under guard, but at sea they leave us alone there."

"In ones and twos," Bolan warned. "If you draw attention from the men holding this ship, all of you may be killed."

"They can't sail the ship without us," Kirinov said. "They threaten and they bluster, but they know we are all needed."

"If they're just wanting to connect with the purchaser," Bolan pointed out, "those men probably don't care if this ship finishes this voyage."

"We'll do as you say," Kirinov promised.

Bolan wished the men luck, then turned his attention to the prow.

"Letting those men go could be a mistake," Price said over the radio.

"There are innocents on board," Bolan told her. "The first order of business is to get them clear. They can do that better than I can because they know the ship. And if they get caught, they might be able to finesse the situation. I can't. This way I get two jobs done at the same time."

Price didn't say anything more.

The Executioner worked quickly and expertly. The job on the prow didn't have to be pretty, just effective. After embedding the remote-control detonators, he checked the arming frequencies, then added timers, as well as a backup. He set them for twenty minutes. If the play got busted and he was caught, downed or the frequencies somehow got jammed, the backup timers would still hole the ship.

"I've got a Special Forces detachment headed your way," Price said.

Bolan crossed the hold back to the two dead men. "What's their ETA?"

"Fifteen minutes. They'll be deplaning and descending by parachute. If we're lucky, we'll all be in and out before Indian air units scramble to check out the action. *Charity's Smile* is currently skating the line between national and international waters."

Checking his watch, Bolan said, "They'll have three minutes before this situation goes ballistic."

"They're SEALs," Price replied. "If they haven't gotten control of the ship in three minutes, it's not going to happen."

"Agreed." Bolan stripped the pea coat from the biggest dead man. Blood smeared the fabric, but the coat served to hide his weapons from casual inspection. The makeshift disguise would be even better in the wan moonlight of the upper deck. Slinging the MP-5 from a shoulder strap made the compact machine pistol almost disappear.

He walked back up the stairs, combat senses alert, and climbed through the hatch onto the deck. Nobody challenged him; nobody even seemed to know he was there. Turning, he walked toward the stern, keeping the silenced SIG-Sauer P-226 clenched in his fist inside his jacket pocket. Despite the salt-tainted night air, he smelled the dead man's blood on the fabric.

Fyodor stood with four other men in the shadows of the boom arm. All of the Russian sailors were hard-eyed men. They carried huge wrenches as weapons.

"Who's the captain?" Bolan asked.

A gaunt, gray-haired man dressed in a worn pea coat glanced at Fyodor.

Fyodor nodded. "This is the man, Captain."

Turning back to Bolan, the captain said, "I am Captain Vassily Anikanov. You have set explosives on my ship?"

Bolan nodded.

"How long before—?" The captain couldn't finish.

"Long enough for you to get your men clear," Bolan said.

"This far out into the ocean?" The captain shook his head. "We'll never make shore without help."

"You'll have it."

Anikanov hesitated. "I wish I could believe you."

"I could have killed your two sailors and blown the ship without warning you," Bolan pointed out.

The captain nodded uncomfortably.

"Where's Kirinov?"

"Trying to get the helmsman," the captain said. "If I went after Usenko, these men would know that something was wrong. Kirinov was the logical choice."

"Where are the criminals?"

"There's a small recreational area in the forward berths,"

the captain said. "They're probably watching pornographic videos. They seem to favor that. And drinking."

"How many guards do they post?"

"None posted. They keep two men in the pilothouse to watch whichever among us is on duty, but sometimes they sail the ship themselves. Or, at least, they pretend to. Most of the systems are automated, and this far out there is little danger of running into another ship. They only want to make certain we don't use the ship's radio to broadcast a distress signal. Occasionally some of the men come out to check the deck. But where would we go while we're this far out from land? Entering the sea here would be suicide."

"Staying on this ship is going to be suicide, Captain." Bolan nodded toward the lifeboat sitting across the stern. "At the first sign of trouble, get that lifeboat overboard and follow it into the sea. An American Special Forces team is already en route. They know you're in the area, but they're not going to be picking and choosing who to save when they board this ship."

"I understand."

"Good luck, Captain."

"And to you," the captain replied. "These are very bad men." His eyes narrowed. "I watched them kill my crewmen, men that I served years with. Those were unconscionable acts. I hope you and your comrades kill them all."

Without a word, Bolan turned and started back toward midships. He kept focused on his task, aware that at any moment the men aboard might choose to make one of their haphazard rounds and catch him. But he was also grimly aware that Kirinov might not be able to retrieve the last of the sailors without help.

"Striker, this is Stony Base," Price called.

"Go, Stony Base," Bolan replied.

"We're picking up three bogeys zeroing in on your position from the north, northeast."

Bolan automatically looked in that direction. Only the double black of the night descending to touch the sea met his gaze. "What are they?"

"Boats," Price replied. "And they're closing fast."

SAENGKEO ZHAO STOOD in the wheelhouse of the powerboat and gazed through the spray breaking across the vessel's prow. She watched the tracking device the boat's pilot used to locate the Russian cargo ship that was their target. Rance Stoddard had provided the device, just as the CIA agent provided the information about the ship's location.

Stoddard had claimed that the CIA was tracking a number of suspect ships in the area, but without conclusive proof that the nuclear weapon was on board, the American agents couldn't act. Saengkeo didn't believe Stoddard's claims about tracking the ship back to a rendezvous with the other Russian ship, *Jadviga,* and believed that the man's knowledge of *Charity's Smile* was more likely the result of an informer selling out to the CIA.

After getting the information from Stoddard, Saengkeo had arranged the interception. A cargo ship owned by one of the Moon Shadow triad's legitimate companies in Singapore had stored the three powerboats they now used to overtake *Charity's Smile.* Johnny Kwan had organized the strike force team, drawing from the best men they had that still stalked the violent shadows around the triad. Together, Saengkeo and Kwan had taken a helicopter from Hong Kong and joined the cargo ship at sea.

Kwan stood at her side, holding light-multiplying binoculars to his eyes.

"Is there any sign of the airplane Stoddard reported?" Saengkeo asked.

"No," Kwan answered.

Only a few minutes earlier, the CIA agent had reported the presence of an unidentified aircraft. Since the plane was slow moving, Stoddard had reasoned that the aircraft might be there to pick up the nuclear warhead. He'd insisted that they set out at once instead of waiting any longer. Saengkeo hadn't liked being pressed. Even equipped with extra fuel tanks, the three powerboats were going to be hard-pressed to return to the cargo ship functioning as a supply station for them.

According to Stoddard's report, the airplane had never gotten closer than a half mile to the cargo ship. Maybe negotiations were still under way.

Clad in a skintight blacksuit and wearing a Kevlar vest, Saengkeo carried her Walther pistols in their shoulder rig and a Kalashnikov AKSU. A transceiver in her right ear, channeled through relays aboard the powerboats, kept her in touch with her team. She glanced back at the men Kwan had chosen.

All of the men were hard-eyed, lean and ready. They were commandos, the best of the best among the Moon Shadows, trained by Johnny Kwan and martial-arts instructors Kwan had selected. All of them wore black, as she did, and also carried Kalashnikovs.

"We're being hailed," the man at the wheel said. "The cargo ship wants to know who we are."

Kwan glanced at her. "In the open water like this, there is no way to disguise our intentions."

Saengkeo stepped closer to the radio and turned up the volume. She heard a man's voice speaking in Russian. "Answer him," she instructed. "Tell him they can surrender peacefully or we will kill every person on board."

Stoddard had been emphatic about that part of the operation, that everyone aboard the ship was a potential enemy. The CIA agent wanted no witnesses to talk about what had happened.

The pilot cupped the microphone in his hand and spoke

rapidly in Russian. As he spoke, the three powerboats closed on the cargo ship like hawks swooping in on vulnerable prey.

HIDDEN IN THE SHADOWS outside the wheelhouse, the Executioner listened to the exchange over the radio. He held the sound-suppressed SIG-Sauer P-226 before him.

"Surrender your ship," a man's voice ordered in Russian over the radio. "If you don't, we will board you and kill everyone."

Someone inside the wheelhouse cursed, then said, "Go wake Viktor! Tell him what is going on!"

Bolan glanced at the dive watch. Eleven minutes remained until the SEALs arrived; fourteen minutes remained until the C-4 blew.

"Stony Base, have you identified the bogeys?" Bolan asked.

"Negative, Striker. Our satellite patch-through access won't allow us the fine imaging we'd need for that."

"How far out are they?"

"At their present rate of speed, one minute and closing. They're not wasting any time."

"I've got your back door, Striker," Grimaldi added. "Give a yell and I'll come running." The Albatross was armed with light machine guns.

Bolan didn't hesitate. Kirinov and the other man, Usenko, needed to be clear of the situation if he could get them that way. The Executioner listened as footsteps rang on the metallic deck and pounded toward him. Spinning around the corner, the warrior aimed the SIG-Sauer down at the center of the man's face less than five feet away.

The man froze. He was dressed like the other sailors aboard *Charity's Smile,* but he brought up a Tokarev pistol a heartbeat too slowly.

Bolan stroked the P-226's trigger twice, putting both subsonic rounds into the center of the man's face. Slammed back by the hollowpoint bullets, the man dropped to the floor.

Kirinov stood near a young man that Bolan assumed was Usenko.

Two other armed guards occupied the wheelhouse. Both of them went for their weapons, moving automatically to take cover behind the Russian sailors.

"Down!" Bolan ordered, tracking the men with the P-226.

Kirinov reached for the younger man, grabbing a double fistful of his jacket, then lunging and dragging both of them from their feet. They fell even as the two guards opened fire.

The deafening blasts of gunfire filled the wheelhouse. One of the men reached out and slapped a button on the control panel in front of him. Immediately the harsh roar of a Klaxon screamed through the night.

Coolly Bolan put the P-226's sights on the chest of the man on the left, and fired four times. Three of the rounds hit the man, turning him, allowing the fourth round to skate past and strike the control panel. Sparks leaped in the wake of the bullet, making miniature lightning in the darkened room.

Even as the man fell and Bolan was switching to his next target, the guard fired again, the blossom of the muzzle-flash lighting his features. The Executioner squeezed the trigger, then felt a sledgehammer slap against his chest, knocking him backward. Pain filled his conscious mind. Unable to breathe, unable to stand, Bolan went down.

4

The earsplitting detonations carried over the open radio channel and echoed inside the powerboat's cabin. Saengkeo Zhao looked at Johnny Kwan, seeking confirmation although she was certain she'd identified what the thunderclaps had been.

"That was gunfire," Kwan said, lifting his binoculars.

For a moment, Saengkeo thought perhaps the men aboard the merchant ship were firing at the three powerboats. She raked the cargo vessel with her gaze but spotted no distinctive muzzle-flashes that would have been present if the men had fired on them.

"Someone is aboard the ship," she said.

Kwan nodded.

"Do you see anything?" Saengkeo asked.

"No."

Turning over the possibilities in her mind, Saengkeo weighed her options.

"If we are going to do this," Kwan said calmly, reaching out to switch off the radio that still carried echoes of the mysterious blasts of gunfire, "we'd be better off doing this quickly."

Remembering how her brother had been killed getting one of the nuclear warheads for the Americans, Saengkeo looked forward to the coming confrontation. But at the same time, she realized getting the weapon back for Stoddard was suddenly a risk. There were probably other teams closing in at the same time.

Failing to recover the nuclear weapon would be unacceptable to Stoddard. And if she failed, would the American lobby against her, against the plans that were under way to free her family from the triads? She didn't know. Failure, therefore, wasn't an option.

Saengkeo looked at the pilot. "Take us in."

Turning abruptly and walking toward the waiting commandos, Saengkeo spoke over the ear transceiver. "Chow."

"Yes," the man replied.

"Hold your boat to starboard with us and provide covering fire as we board."

"Yes."

"Sing, take your boat to stern. Watch to see if the crew tries to throw the cargo overboard for later recovery."

Saengkeo turned to Kwan. "I want that ship."

"STRIKER!"

For a moment, black comets spun in Bolan's vision. His lungs felt as though they had locked up and weren't going to function again. Despite the Kevlar vest that had prevented the bullet from penetrating his heart, the sheer blunt trauma of the round striking had knocked the breath from the warrior's lungs and nearly caused him to pass out.

"Striker, you've got a gunner coming down on your twenty!"

Galvanized by Price's words cutting through the fog filling his brain, Bolan opened his eyes and tracked the movement he saw in his peripheral vision.

Bullets cut the air above Bolan as the *mafiya* shooter fired.

The Executioner raised the P-226 and squeezed off rounds as quickly as he could, aiming for the center of the muzzle-flashes. Two of the 9 mm rounds flamed the railing beside the enemy gunner, but the others struck him, breaking his stride and clubbing him backward. Bolan didn't stop firing until the pistol cycled dry.

His breath returned to him in a rush. Pushing himself to his feet, he glanced at Kirinov and Usenko in the wheelhouse. Dumping the empty magazine from the SIG-Sauer and ramming a fresh one home, Bolan waved the two sailors on.

The Russians raced for the door.

Bolan sheathed the P-226 and shrugged out of the pea coat. The time for disguises had passed. He slid the MP-5 from his shoulder, watching as men rushed to the deck. The Executioner swept a blistering figure eight at them, knocking one down and driving the others to cover.

"Go!" Bolan yelled at Kirinov, shoving both men toward the stern. "Captain Anikanov has a lifeboat waiting."

Kirinov kept a grip on the younger man and hustled him toward the stern.

"Stony Base," Bolan called, keeping up covering fire to protect the retreating sailors, "verify five men down, eleven up."

"Affirmative," Price replied. "Stony Base verifies five down, zero chance of return to battle. Eleven up. All eleven are forward of your position." The thermographic ability of the satellite the Stony Man intelligence team had logged onto provided the tactical information.

"Acknowledged," Bolan replied. He was the thin line separating the relatively unarmed Russian sailors from the *mafiya.* "Where are the bogeys?" He checked the video camera buckled over his heart and saw the smear of the deflected bullet less than an inch from the device. Knowing the camera could catch a lot that he might not see at the moment and could be used during a later debrief, he switched the device on.

"On top of you," Price replied. "To starboard."

As if in response to the mission controller's announcement, one of the *mafiya* gunners standing by the starboard railing suddenly jerked to port, hurled by a blast heralded by the unmistakable roar of a Kalashnikov on full-auto.

"How many bogeys?" Bolan asked.

"Dozens, Striker. We haven't been able to sort them all out. Three boatloads. There's no chance of your holding that position till the backup teams arrive."

Bolan ducked behind one of the tarp-covered stacks of crates lashed to the midships decks. "Are the backup teams ready to work the recovery when I put this ship down?" He shoved a fresh magazine into the MP-5.

"They've got access to deep-sea submersibles that can be deployed within the hour. No one else will get to the cargo first."

Bolan nodded and peered around the corner of the crate stack. "Acknowledged, Stony Base. Let the backup teams know I'm putting this ship down."

"Already done, Striker."

As Bolan watched, two *mafiya* gunners broke cover and rushed his position, thinking perhaps that he had abandoned cover. Swinging out the MP-5's muzzle, the Executioner triggered a fusillade of bullets that chewed through both men waist high. Seven down aboard the cargo ship, Bolan thought, but dozens coming.

A line flew over the starboard railing, was quickly pulled through and a rope ladder followed, pulled up on the line. Almost instantly, black-clad warriors climbed to the deck, blasting away at the gunners trapped between their own murderous fire and Bolan's marksmanship.

Ripping an antipersonnel grenade from his combat harness, Bolan slipped the spoon, counted a quick two-count, then flung the grenade. The bomb bounced against the metal deck and skidded toward the prow. Bolan pulled back to cover, not wanting to lose his night vision.

The grenade detonated almost immediately. The pellets released by the explosion rattled against the metal floor and bulkhead, followed by the hoarse and frightened cries of wounded and dying men.

Glancing around the stack of crates, Bolan saw two bodies, one of them Asian, sprawled over the deck in growing pools of blood. Bullets slapped the crates he took cover behind, ripping the wood and sending splinters pinwheeling into the air like confetti. He took another grenade, this one a smoker, and heaved the explosive toward the prow.

Other arriving Asian gunners took cover, expecting another antipersonnel grenade. An instant later, the grenade went off, throwing out a cloud of black smoke that obscured that section of the ship.

Confident in the smoke screen, Bolan left his position and sprinted to the stern. Before he blew the C-4, he wanted to give the Russian sailors every chance to clear the ship.

When the warrior found the sailors, he also found they were pinned down by enemy fire from a powerboat trailing in the cargo ship's stern wake. A powerful searchlight sliced across the deck, chasing the shadows. All of the sailors lay hunkered down across the deck. One man was dead, his face blown apart by gunfire.

Captain Anikanov, one shoulder bloody and his face racked with pain, looked up at Bolan helplessly. "We can't get to the lifeboat, and we don't stand a chance in the sea without it."

Bolan silently agreed. He crawled to the edge of the stern,

avoiding the searchlight by staying below the angle of the sweeps. Remaining prone, the warrior changed hands with the machine pistol and drew the Desert Eagle.

The powerboat was almost fifty yards behind the cargo ship.

Sighting deliberately, resting his right forearm over his left, knowing that the men boarding the ship would be on him in a moment, the Executioner squeezed the Desert Eagle's trigger as relentlessly as a metronome. The big .44 Magnum pistol bounced in his fist, and as soon as he rode out the recoil, he brought the sights to bear on the steering section again and again.

Abruptly, the powerboat veered away.

Bolan didn't know if he'd hit the pilot or if the pilot had chosen discretion as the better part of valor. He holstered and slung his weapons and stood.

"Man the ropes," the Executioner ordered. "Heave the lifeboat over." He grabbed the nearest rope holding the lifeboat in place and started hauling.

Captain Anikanov ordered his men to help. Once the ropes were manned, the lifeboat rose from the moorings in a rush. The spinning pulleys sang overhead, even louder than the gunfire continuing to come from *Charity's Smile*'s prow. At the apex of the lifeboat's climb, shots sparked from the pulleys and the boat stopped moving.

"She's locked up," Kirinov called out. "One of the pulleys was jammed by the gunfire."

In the next instant, a new wave of gunfire came from the powerboat returning to the cargo ship's stern. Kirinov was hit, sent spinning away, and the rest of the Russian sailors dropped to the deck again.

Having no choice, Bolan followed them.

SAENGKEO ZHAO STARED incredulously for a moment at the corpse draped across the top of the powerboat. The dead man lay on his back, showing the gory ruin that remained of his face after the grenade had gone off on the cargo ship's deck.

Death had come in a heartbeat.

"Saengkeo," Kwan called.

Kwan stood in the last of the billowing black smoke that had covered the deck. Another man held the bottom of the rope ladder as the powerboat pilot held the vessel steady, matching the cargo ship's speed.

Saengkeo grabbed the rope ladder and went up almost effortlessly in spite of the way she was slung and banged against the cargo ship's hull. Once on deck, she held her assault rifle at the ready.

"Are any of the *mafiya* men alive?" she asked. The vestiges of the smoke burned her eyes, nose and throat.

"We have a prisoner," Kwan confirmed.

"Where?"

Kwan led her to the front of the wheelhouse so they would be protected from enemy fire coming from the rear of the ship.

Two of Kwan's men held the Russian against the bulkhead. "Where is the nuclear weapon?" Saengkeo demanded.

"Fuck you!" the man said.

Without a word, moving so fast the man didn't even have time to react, Saengkeo slipped a throwing knife from her sleeve. She grabbed the man's right ear in her left hand and sliced it from his head.

The man howled in pain and shocked disbelief. He struggled against the two men that held him, but they pinned him against the bulkhead.

Saengkeo showed the man his ear, dangling the piece of flesh from her fingertips. "You have another ear," she said. She allowed him no mercy, knowing that the man had probably done things just as bad to people who were true victims. She blocked all thought of mercy and compassion, thinking only of the children growing up in Hong Kong in the shadows of the triads.

"Belowdecks," the man yelled as blood streamed down the side of his face and covered his shoulder. "The warhead is belowdecks. In the cargo hold."

"Show me," Saengkeo said, stepping back and nodding to the two men. The wound wasn't debilitating despite the damage, and there was no danger the man would bleed out before the blood coagulated.

Stumbling, one hand clapped to the side of his head, blood streaming from between his fingers, the man walked back to amidships. He stepped over the bodies of his dead companions, gazing at them in stunned fascination and disbelief.

"How many men are aboard ship?" Saengkeo asked.

"All we have seen is one," Kwan answered. "He's back there with a group of sailors from this ship."

"Mafiya?"

"No. They are genuine sailors. It appears that the *mafiya* team kept on part of the original crew to run the ship. They were trying to get off the ship with a lifeboat, but we have managed to prevent that."

Glancing to the stern of the ship, Saengkeo saw the lifeboat suspended in midair. "Sing," she said.

"Yes," Sing replied over the transceiver.

"I don't want any of those men to leave this ship."

"No one will leave."

The *mafiya* man went down into the cargo hold, followed by the team that Kwan assigned to him. Saengkeo remained topside with Kwan, her thoughts tumbling over one another like a stream sluicing over a dam, wondering if the men she was fighting now were the men who had killed her brother. None of the *mafiya* gunners seemed good enough. Syn-Tek had been much too clever, much too fast for men like the ones on the boat.

But the man dressed in black she had seen moving across the ship's deck before the grenade explosion, that man had seemed different. He was deadly and dangerous, fearless in the face of death.

"We found the warhead," one of Kwan's men called over the radio.

Still taking cover by the cargo hold, Saengkeo peered down into the ship. She spotted the Russian and Kwan's team against the stern bulkhead. Together, they pried up a section of the flooring. In the next instant, a blinding flash filled the cargo hold. Struggling with her vision, her head pierced by a blinding headache, Saengkeo watched as the crates from the prow of the ship suddenly hurtled toward the stern, followed by a roiling wall of flames.

Charity's Smile reeled without warning, shuddering deeply down in her guts. She suddenly rode the water all wrong. The ship was dying, and Saengkeo had been aboard enough ships to know that.

Spots marred Saengkeo's vision, but she could see clearly enough to note the water suddenly spewing into the cargo hold from the huge rupture in the ship's prow. Flotsam and debris were already floating on two or three feet of water that was rapidly rising inside the cargo bay. Corpses of the men who had been in the hold were floating, as well.

"He mined the ship," Kwan said.

Saengkeo stared at the rising water. "We could still get the warhead."

Kwan shook his head. "There's not enough time. Maybe minutes, but probably less. The warhead is too heavy, too hard to handle. If we don't get off this ship quickly, we could be sucked down with the undertow."

Fear thudded through Saengkeo's heart. They had been so close, only to have their prize ripped from their fingers—the prize ripped from her *family*. She looked at Kwan. "I want that man dead. We have time enough for that. And he has nowhere to go with the lifeboat hanging in the rigging like that."

BOLAN THREW AWAY the remote-control detonator and leaned back against the stack of crates as return fire suddenly heated up. Evidently the triad troops knew who to blame for the explosion. He stared up at the lifeboat suspended overhead, caught up in the rigging.

"You have set off the explosives," Captain Anikanov said.

"Yeah," Bolan said.

"Then you have killed us all." There was no accusation in the old man's words, but there was no hope, either. "We're never getting off this ship."

"We're getting off the ship," Bolan replied. "Knight, do you read me?"

"Fly-By Knight reads you five by five, Striker," Grimaldi replied.

"Ready for a piece of the action?"

"I'm on my way."

Bolan jarred against the stack of crates at his back as the ship wallowed unexpectedly. *Charity's Smile* rode more slowly in the water, approaching a dead stop as her cargo hold filled with water. The deck listed now, rolling to port and having a definite downward tilt. She was going down fast.

"I need you to take out the powerboat following astern the ship," Bolan said. "I've still got a crew of sailors to get off board and we're pinned down."

"Acknowledged, Striker. Fly-By Knight is winging your way."

"Stony Base," Bolan said.

"Go, Striker."

"What about your troops?"

"Only seven minutes away."

And the way the warrior measured time in a battle, seven minutes was a lifetime. Several lifetimes in fact, he amended as he glanced at the Russian sailors.

Bolan peered around the corner of the stack and zipped a triburst into one of the Asian men's chest and a second triburst into his head. There was no sign of the woman he'd seen earlier. Plucking a frag grenade from his combat harness, he pulled the pin and tossed the grenade out onto the deck.

The explosion blew shot all over the deck.

In the next instant, the Albatross appeared in the sky, too far out and coming too fast for her prop roar to be heard.

"Striker, I'm coming through." Grimaldi opened with a short machine-gun salvo that strafed the prow deck and knocked down triad gunners.

Knowing that everyone aboard the ship would have their attention on the approaching airplane, Bolan stood briefly and grabbed the three ropes that held the lifeboat with working pulleys. He looped the ropes under the steel railing, hoping that the metal would hold the sudden weight.

A light smattering of gunfire chased the warrior back down to the deck, but he maintained his hold on the ropes. "Here," he said to Anikanov. "Have your men pull on these ropes. They run under the lifeboat above."

Anikanov looked up. Understanding dawned in his eyes.

The Albatross dived out of the sky like a diving falcon, attracting enemy gunfire almost at once. Then Grimaldi fired his guns again, unleashing twin lines of purple tracers that burned across a brief patch of the sea until he had a target lock. The twin 7.62 mm light machine guns hammered the powerboat, tracking across the fuel tanks.

Grimaldi was only a short distance out and fifty feet above sea level when the tracer rounds ignited the volatile fuel carried aboard the powerboat. The boat exploded, vaporizing as a series of detonations erupted on board. Flaming kindling blew into the sky, and the Albatross flew through the fire. Flames clung to the aircraft for a time, but were quickly whisked away by the wind.

"Clear," Grimaldi said.

"Affirmative," Bolan replied.

He glanced at the sailors and switched to Russian. "Pull!"

When the lines under the lifeboat grew taut, taking up some of the boat's weight, the Executioner fired at the ropes above the pulleys. The rounds sliced through the ropes, releasing the lifeboat in a staggered fall. The sailors struggled with the lifeboat's weight but hung on grimly, knowing the boat was their only chance.

The lifeboat coasted down the ropes, following the lines over the edge of the stern railing, then dropped into the white-capped wake behind the cargo ship.

"Go," Bolan ordered, slipping a fresh magazine into the MP-5.

Captain Anikanov rallied at once, ordering his men overboard, shoving the ones ahead who didn't move quickly enough. Fyodor paused long enough to help Kirinov to his feet. Together, the two old sailors stumbled toward the railing and fell overboard.

"Striker," Price called, "the backup teams are only three minutes out. We don't have a cover story in play for you."

"Acknowledged," Bolan replied. The arriving SEALs were a danger to him. If they arrived and caught him on-site, he'd be taken down along with the triad gunners. And if he survived, they'd take him captive, ID him for who he was, and he'd be in a federal prison in a heartbeat for the long list of crimes that he was wanted for in several countries.

The Executioner yanked a frag grenade from his harness, spun and threw the explosive toward the prow. The grenade skipped across the metal deck and blew, throwing antipersonnel shot in all directions.

The triad gunners stepped up return fire. For a moment, the Executioner caught sight of the woman as she broke cover and raced forward. Bolan tapped the MP-5's trigger, delivering a 3-round burst that caught the woman across the chest and knocked her down.

The bullets didn't kill her, though. She pulled herself to cover behind a stack of crates as Bolan's next rounds scored the metal deck. He wheeled to reload, glancing back behind the vessel to see the Russian crewmen scrambling aboard the lifeboat. The cargo ship still continued forward slowly, increasing distance from the lifeboat.

"Stony Base, did you apprise the backup team of possible friendlies on-site?" Bolan asked.

"Affirmative, Striker. That intel is working through channels even as we speak. Those men will be taken care of."

The cargo ship lurched again, throwing everyone off balance for a moment.

Bolan peered around the corner of the crates where he took cover, spotted the cargo straps holding the crates in place ahead of him and opened up with the MP-5. The lockdown cleats jerked and snapped off as the 9 mm rounds hammered them.

When the ship caught another bad roll, the cargo lines jerked, then pulled free. Tons of cargo spilled across the deck, becoming an avalanche that rolled toward the prow and the triad gunners.

For good measure, Bolan pulled the pins on his last three grenades, two frags and a smoker, and heaved them forward. The explosives bounced but got caught up in the scattered cargo.

Pushing himself to his feet, taking advantage of the situation, the Executioner sprinted for the cargo ship's stern. He drove his feet hard, keeping his head low and hoping any gunners recovering quickly would aim at his back where the Kevlar would protect him.

The grenades went off, unleashing more destruction and a confusion of smoke clouds.

"Fly-By Knight," Bolan called as he leaped over the cargo ship's stern.

"I see you, Striker," Grimaldi called out. "I see you. Just go deep and swim straight out. I'll put the bird down on the water and pick you up in just a minute."

Bolan put both hands in front of him, holding the MP-5 canted so the machine pistol wouldn't resist the impact as much. He punched through the sea surface and felt the cold water close over his head.

STOMACH AND SIDE ACHING from the bullets that had flattened against her Kevlar vest, Saengkeo was buffeted before a large wooden crate skidding across the deck. The crate screeched across the metal surface, hammering her again and again.

Finally the cargo ship righted somewhat and allowed her to shove away from the crate. She didn't feel too badly about the experience, though, because the crate had saved her from the frag grenade's payload that had taken out the man standing next to her.

She forced herself to her feet, sipping breaths because a full lung expansion hurt. Glancing at Kwan, who was getting to his own feet nearby, she asked, "Where is the man?" Both of them knew what man she was talking about.

"He went over the stern," Kwan replied.

Abruptly radio feedback echoed in Saengkeo's ear. For a moment, she thought the transceiver had been damaged in the succession of blasts or while she'd been thrown around on the deck.

Then Stoddard's voice came over the frequency, sounding as if he were speaking out of a well. "Get clear of the area. There are American military forces en route to your position. Your getting caught there won't do any of us any good."

"American military forces?" Saengkeo demanded. "You didn't know about them?"

"Military isn't the same as CIA," Stoddard replied. "The operate their own agenda. I knew they were in the area, but I didn't know they were aware of this ship. Evidently, the fighting on board *Charity's Smile* drew their attention."

Reaching the stern section of the sinking ship, Saengkeo stared out at the sea. Flaming debris from the powerboat that had been destroyed still floated in small islands, warring against the darkness and the insistent ocean. "What about the man that led the attack here?"

Stoddard was silent just for a moment. "I don't know. I'm going to try to identify him." He raised his voice. "Get off the ship."

Still, Saengkeo stood and stared out at the black, rolling sea. She saw the Albatross drop from the sky, almost coming to a full stop in midair before dropping to the water. The rounded hull glided across the water, balanced by the wing pontoons.

The plane's running lights illuminated the dark water, peeling back the night's shadows to reveal the man in the water nearby. As Saengkeo watched, the man lifted an arm and caught the aircraft's wing in passing. The plane continued forward, pulling the man up out of the water. With a lithe move, he yanked himself up onto the wing, then made his way to the cargo door.

The airplane's props turned faster, churning up silvery foam in the craft's wake. A moment later, the aircraft lifted into the air.

"Saengkeo," Kwan called.

Staring up at the plane lifting above the ocean, Saengkeo thought about her murdered brother and the men who had been killed trying to take the Russian freighter. "This," she said to the man in the plane, "is not over. I will find you, and I will kill you when I do."

Then she turned and followed Johnny Kwan from the ship.

MACK BOLAN STARED down through light-multiplying binoculars at the sinking Russian freighter and watched as the Asian strike-force team boarded the two powerboats. He pulled on the headset Grimaldi offered.

"Striker," Barbara Price said over the frequency.

"Yeah," Bolan replied. He loosened the Kevlar vest and felt the violent pain across his chest where the bullets had hammered him mercilessly. He was going to be bruised for days.

"We've IDed the woman on board the cargo ship," Price said.

"Saengkeo Zhao," Bolan replied, watching the woman as she scrambled aboard one of the powerboats. "Leader of the Moon Shadow triad."

"You saw her."

"Up close," Bolan agreed. "How did she get there?"

"I don't know."

"We need to find out. She's got too many ties to the missing packages."

"Agreed. We'll be working on it."

Bolan watched the powerboats speed away from the sinking freighter, which barely remained above the ocean's surface. "What about the freighter crew?" He glanced to the north and spotted the lifeboat riding the waves.

"We're keeping an eye on them. The arriving Special Forces will take them in and give them safe passage to a friendly harbor."

Bolan glanced at Grimaldi. "Any chance of overtaking the powerboats?"

"Sure," Grimaldi replied. "But we'd be like the dog chasing a car. What are we gonna do with them when we catch them? I'm blown on ammunition." He paused and shot Bolan a quick glance. "Unless you want to take them on with small arms. The fuel situation's getting critical, too. I'm all up for the underdog route, Sarge. Hell, we mapped the freeway. But that long swim back could be a killer."

Bolan didn't even give the possibility thought. He leaned back in the copilot's seat. Water seeped from his clothing and chilled him despite the heater blowing into the cockpit. "Let them go. If she was out here tonight, Jack, Saengkeo is part of this."

He looked through the binoculars again. "Stony Base."

"Go, Striker."

"I need a target of opportunity," the Executioner said. He stared down through the binoculars and discovered that the woman was staring up at him through binoculars of her own.

"What do you suggest?"

"I want something away from Hong Kong," Bolan said. "Holdings that belong to the Moon Shadows. I want to rattle the cages and see if we can draw the woman out into the open."

"Then you'll want to make for Vancouver, British Columbia," Price replied. "A lot of new Moon Shadow business has shown up there over the past few years. Most of those businesses are legal, but there are some high-yield cash cows among them that could hurt or cripple the organization financially."

"Fine." The woman and the powerboat passed from Bolan's sight. He swept the ocean again, spotting the lifeboat but not the stricken freighter. "I don't see the ship."

"It's under," Price said. "But the Special Forces group has the area mapped. If they don't make the recovery tonight, it'll happen within hours."

"Still leaves one more package."

"I know. I've got to make some phone calls and put together a package for you in Canada. If I find anything out, I'll call."

"Thanks." Bolan listened to the connection break. He stared at the ghostly reflections in the windows caused by the glowing instrumentation. Grimaldi knew the big warrior well enough to give him time alone.

The Executioner moved the pieces around in his mind, matching known players to understandable motives. Evidently Saengkeo Zhao's part in unfolding events was larger than anyone had guessed. Or maybe the woman was seeking to capitalize on information she'd gotten through some avenue open to her. However she'd gotten the information, she appeared set on recovering the nukes. Two were down. One was in American hands, and the second soon to be if Price's intel was on the mark, and Bolan was willing to believe the mission controller.

But what about the third?

Bolan leaned back in the seat and breathed deeply, testing the bruised muscle across his chest where the Kevlar had stopped the bullets. So far, he'd been trailing the operation, a step behind the major plays. But that was all about to change.

The Executioner was going on the offensive. He had an enemy in his sights now, and he intended to lay a hellzone right in the heart of Moon Shadow territory.

5

Vancouver, British Columbia

Nightlife in Vancouver, British Columbia, was thriving. Flashing lights and neon lit up the downtown sector, but death lay masked in the shadows. Colors from garish neon lights danced on the waters of Burrard Inlet, warring with the running lights of pleasure ships and the clubs that lined the waterfront. Farther out, fog dimmed the view of the part of the city on the other side of the inlet.

Dark clouds obscured the moon and promised rain to accompany the brisk, cool wind that blew in from Coal Harbour to the north. Traffic noises drifted up from the street. Cars filled the thoroughfares and pedestrians filled the sidewalks and nightclubs.

Mack Bolan stood hidden in the shadows on the building rooftop across the street from the Nautilus Club.

"Striker," Barbara Price called over the ear-throat collar communicator the soldier wore.

"Copy, Stony Base," the Executioner responded. A geo-

synchronous satellite conducted communications from Stony
Man Farm in the United States to British Columbia. The
cutouts Aaron Kurtzman had rigged up for the night in case
of an interception would show the communications originat-
ing in Los Angeles. Even a professional with a Vegas-break-
ing lucky streak couldn't track the signal to the hardsite in the
Blue Ridge Mountains.

"Confirm target's location," Price said. "Turning off West
Hastings onto Howe Street."

Bolan lifted the micro-Bushnell light-amplifying binoculars he'd brought for the night's mission. He raked the
street with his gaze. Howe Street was a one-way avenue that
brought traffic deeper into the heart of the city. The next
street up was Hornby Street, and it was one-way in the other
direction, leading to Canada Place and the Sea Bus terminal.

At the corner, a bright yellow-and-black Corvette con-
vertible turned onto Howe from West Hastings. The raised
black vinyl top blocked view of the driver.

"Can't confirm the target," Bolan replied. He checked the
license plates as the car pulled into the valet parking space in
front of the Nautilus Club. "Vehicle ID confirmed."

"Acknowledged," Price said. "According to the intel we
have, no one else drives that car. We made the surveillance
tag on the target's cell phone from inside the car. Less than
two minutes passed before we were able to lock on to a visual of the vehicle."

Bolan studied the vehicle as a valet strode forward and
opened the driver's door. The driver was tall and lanky. Neon
lights from the Nautilus Club gleamed against his shaved
head and from his dangling earring and necklace. Fierce tattoos marked the driver's arms. He started for the club's doors
without looking at the valet.

"Confirm target," Bolan said.

"Acknowledged," Price responded. "You and Mustang are solo inside the building. We'll only be able to offer limited help at this end."

"Affirmative, Stony Base. Striker has the ball." Bolan watched his quarry enter the Nautilus Club. "Mustang, do you copy?"

"Mustang copies," Jack Grimaldi answered.

"Identify and verify," Bolan requested.

"Affirmative, Striker. Back to you in a short."

Shifting, Bolan stood, trusting the darkness atop the building and his blacksuit to render him invisible. Fatigue from the trans-Pacific flight that had brought Grimaldi and him to British Columbia from Singapore two days ago still plagued him. The bruises on his chest from the blunt trauma of bullets slamming his Kevlar vest during the shipboard battle on *Charity's Smile* hadn't healed. Thankfully they didn't slow him, either. A professional soldier got used to pain. Pain was a friend, keeping a warrior cognizant of the fact that he was alive and was mortal.

The Executioner reached for his duffel bag. The compressed-air cannon looked like an oversize spear gun. Charged with CO_2 canisters, the air cannon was capable of delivering a barbed spear the length of a football field with only slight noise. The soldier slipped one of the specially made quarrels from the duffel and loaded the cannon. The spool of ultrathin cable he attached to the cannon's stock and the quarrel tested up to three thousand pounds.

With patience born of experience from thousands of war zone assaults, Bolan waited. He had moved the battlefront of his latest engagement to British Columbia because he'd wanted to explore the Moon Shadow triad's weaknesses. Con-

fronting the man who had entered the Nautilus Club was only
the first step in that engagement.

SEATED AT THE BAR inside the Nautilus Club, Jack Grimaldi
nursed a beer and watched a baseball game on one of the ceil-
ing-mounted televisions. During the game, Grimaldi had also
kept track of the arrival of three men known to associate with
Eric Barnes. One of them was an ex-member of the Vancouver Police Department, whose eyes constantly roved over the
club patrons. His name was Harvey Dobbins, but he looked
like an overweight sports jock in casual wear. While working
law enforcement, Dobbins had been part of the Asian Crime
Task Force based in Vancouver but cooperating with similar
departments in the United States. Dobbins had fallen a long
way, drawn by the money that could be made working the dark
streets.

The other two men, one black and one Asian, had rap
sheets that skirted all around a solid, long-term fall, but that
was only because the bodies hadn't been found. Both, the reports from Stony Man Farm indicated, were stone-cold killers.

Grimaldi wore khaki pants, a gray sweater and a brown
leather flight jacket. His nondescript looks and slight build
blended him into the heavy club crowd. He wore an earplug
that was both receiver and transceiver.

The decor of the Nautilus Club consisted of maritime
themes. Traditional nets, oars, fishing rods and ships' wheels
hung from the ceiling and on the walls.

A huge saltwater tank occupied the wall behind the semi-
circle of the mahogany bar, which was the most impressive
piece in the place. Sea horses clung to long strands of sea-
weed and kelp by their tails. Oysters sat on the light tan sand.

Brightly colored fish darted through the water, drawing the eye.

Seated at the bar as he was, Grimaldi had a clear view of the club's main entrance through the reflection presented on the saltwater tank. The ace pilot had been on several missions with the Executioner and was no stranger to stakeouts. Judging from the miserable weather in the area, he figured he had the easy part of the current effort.

"Another beer?" The female bartender wore professional black slacks and a white blouse open enough to reveal a promising amount of freckled cleavage. The shirtsleeves were rolled up to midforearm. Her chestnut hair was cut short and fell to the corner of her mouth.

Looking at the empty glass in his hands, Grimaldi said, "Sure."

The bartender got a fresh glass and stood at the tap. "Want a head on it?"

Grimaldi held his thumb and forefinger a half inch apart. "A little head."

The woman smiled as she put the glass in front of Grimaldi. "A little head," she said, "makes us all happy."

Grimaldi gazed into the woman's blue eyes and grinned. "Are you hitting on me?"

The bartender looked at him demurely. "That wouldn't be very professional, now, would it?"

Grimaldi shook his head. "No."

"But I get off at two. I don't have to be professional then." She slid a cocktail napkin across the bar top. The phone number there was written in a neat hand. Block letters printed SELENA under the number.

"Can't," Grimaldi said.

The bartender raised an eyebrow and glanced at his left hand. "If you're married, you're not wearing a ring."

"Not married. On the job."

A half smile formed on Selena's face. "I didn't take you for a cop."

"Me, neither," Grimaldi agreed. "Private pilot. My boss is one of those dotcom guys. We came up here for a meeting." The story matched the cover Price had engineered from Stony Man Farm.

Selena leaned on the bar top and exposed the cleavage again. "Sounds exciting. Corporate merger? Buyout?"

"Actually he came up here to play a game."

"Poker?"

"Video game," Grimaldi answered.

"I thought they made those down around Seattle after Silicon Valley imploded."

"They do," Grimaldi said. "Contracted the development out up here."

Selena leaned in closer. "I like to play games." She licked her lips. "Role-playing games are my favorite."

A grin spread across Grimaldi's face. The woman was damn hard to ignore. He toasted her with the beer. "I'll bet they are, and I'll bet you're good at them."

"It's a shame you won't be around to find out."

"Yeah," Grimaldi agreed. "Maybe next time."

A man down the bar to Grimaldi's right called for a refill. Selena excused herself from the pilot and walked away, rolling her hips suggestively under the taut black fabric.

Grimaldi made a show of checking the box scores on ESPN, then lifted his glass to cover his mouth. "Striker."

"Go, Mustang," Bolan replied.

"I've got the target." Grimaldi sipped the beer and studied the man they'd come to Vancouver to find.

Eric Barnes stood in the club doorway for just a moment to make a proper entrance. The guy had a healthy respect of his own worth; Grimaldi had to give him that. Then again, Barnes had built up a movie career and a large client list for illegal drugs.

That information had come by way of Price and Kurtzman. They, or someone working the computers at Stony Man Farm, had hacked into Asian Organized Crime offices in Vancouver to get that knowledge.

"Do you know him?" the bartender asked as she returned to Grimaldi.

The pilot knew better than to try to cover by denying that he'd taken notice of Barnes. The bartender was too sharp for that.

"Looks familiar," Grimaldi said. "Guy like that, he tries to get noticed. I thought maybe I'd bumped into him somewhere on the job. My boss does business with a lot of people."

"His name is Eric Barnes," Selena told him. "Local celebrity. He works in the television and movie industry. Gets props, costumes, background stuff to make a warehouse studio lot look like anyplace in the world."

"Has he done anything I'd know about?" Grimaldi asked. Although he looked at the woman, he kept track of Barnes's image in the aquarium glass.

Barnes moved through the club greeting people he knew or pretended to know. The Nautilus Club catered to a late-supper crowd, as well as providing a bar. Most people Barnes talked to appeared glad to see him, but Barnes didn't prolong any of the conversations.

"Eric's done some work for *X-Files* and *Roseanne*." Selena smiled as she watched Barnes. "Some other movies that were done in the area." She shook her head. "Guy really knows how to work a crowd, doesn't he?"

"Yeah," Grimaldi said. "Must come around a lot for all those people to know him."

Selena nodded. "Eric's a regular. He stays in one of the rooms on the sixth floor from time to time. Guess this is one of those times."

"I didn't know there were hotel rooms in this building."

"There aren't any," Selena said. "The first three floors of the building are all shops and restaurants. The next three floors have law offices, travel agencies, telemarketing agencies. And there are some offices left open that rent by the day, by the hour. Eric uses them to impress people he's trying to do business with. A lot of start-up people and shoestring companies do the same."

Grimaldi watched Eric Barnes's reflection stride across the aquarium surface and disappear through a side door near the hallway to the pay phones and bathrooms guarded by the statue of a fishtailed merman holding a trident at present arms.

Dobbins and the two hardcases Grimaldi had identified got up and trailed after Barnes. They stayed just far enough back to avoid attention but close enough to protect Barnes.

The Stony Man pilot squelched the impulse to follow. Bolan was going to close in for the kill. Grimaldi was there to make a positive ID and provide support if he could.

"Mustang," Price said in Grimaldi's ear, "we've lost Barnes. There are too many people in the club to keep track of. We need the tag."

Reaching up, Grimaldi tapped the earplug once in the affirmative, knowing the sound would transmit his recognition of the problem.

"You know," Selena said, "I even heard the upstairs offices have even been used to film X-rated movies. In and out in one day. So to speak."

Grimaldi grinned, ignoring the need to be moving that filled him. "So to speak." He held up the beer and pointed to the bathroom. "Speaking of in and out, I'll be back."

"I'll be here." Selena pushed across the cocktail napkin with her name and number. "You don't want to leave this here. I don't just give that information out to anybody."

Grimaldi palmed the cocktail napkin, then made a show of folding the note and placing it in his bomber jacket pocket. He pushed away from the bar, still carrying the half-full glass of beer.

Hong Kong

"WE'VE GOT a problem."

Irritation and unease grated through Rance Stoddard as he turned from the computer monitors in front of him. He sat in an ergonomic chair that was supposed to be fit for hours spent at a computer terminal. During the past twenty-seven hours, he'd put the time in and the chair was failing.

"I don't need problems," Stoddard snapped. "You've got a good picture of that guy. Get me an ID."

"IDing the guy is the issue," Dave Kelso said. Despite Stoddard's obvious irritation, he remained calm. That skill had been the primary factor in the long relationship they'd maintained in the Asian theater of international politics.

Stoddard pressed his hands together, fingertip to fingertip, and rested his elbows on the chair arms. "You can't ID him."

That wasn't surprising given what he knew about the men he was pursuing. The team consisted of ghosts, had barely left a psychic imprint in Singapore after the incident involving the Russian ship, *Charity's Smile*. CNN still occasionally ran footage of the rescue of the ship's crew, and the follow-up interview with the men who stated pirates had boarded them after they'd been taken over by Russian *mafiya* and forced to carry an undisclosed cargo that was still missing.

He glanced at the bank of monitors that covered the wall in front of him. The office suite was on the twenty-seventh floor of the Bank of China Tower in Hong Kong, but he had people in place in Vancouver, British Columbia.

The two men had abandoned the bullet-riddled amphibious plane in the water off the coast of Singapore. Military naval patrols had recovered the plane, but the two men were gone. Stoddard had called in some heavy favors inside Singapore to ID the two men. They'd paid cash for the aircraft, but the guy who'd sold them the plane had also taken their picture.

When the police had come around, the man had denied knowledge of the two men. Stoddard's people had offered money, which got most secrets out into the open. After the men had gotten the somewhat blurred picture, they'd killed the informant. Stoddard knew the men who bought the plane would be suspect, and the Singapore law-enforcement people were satisfied the men were no longer on the island.

"We can ID the guy," Kelso said. "The problem is, which ID do you want?"

Stoddard pushed the air from his lungs. "How many do you have?"

"So far?" Kelso shrugged. "Upward of three dozen."

"All pilots?"

Kelso nodded. "This guy gets around."

Stoddard stared at the pilot's face on the monitor beside the monitor that showed the interior of the Nautilus Club in Vancouver. The man looked like a nobody, dark hair, dark eyes, Mediterranean features that had been diluted. But there was something dangerous about the man that belied the easy smile on his lips.

The picture of the pilot was from the Nautilus Club. Stoddard had called in more favors in British Columbia.

"What about Jackson Garrett?" Stoddard asked. "Is that his real name?"

"From the cover laid down over his licensing, you'd think so," Kelso said. "Whoever's holding his back, they've got a lot on the info."

"Have you tried breaking the paper trail?"

"First thing," Kelso agreed. "Know what we stirred up?"

"A hornet's nest," Stoddard said bitterly.

"Hell, no," Kelso said. "We're talking about a traveling shitstorm here. I'm using a guy over in Prague to hack the paper trail. Somebody providing the cover sniffed him out, started feeding a virus into his machine in packets that got by his firewall and reduced his hard drive to toast before he ever saw it coming. He's screaming bloody murder and promising Old Testament vengeance, but I don't think he can touch these guys."

"Who is fronting these guys?" Stoddard demanded.

Kelso shook his head and gazed at the live feed coming from British Columbia. "You know this biz as well as I do. Every country out there is coming up to speed in the information wars, and each one of those countries has agencies, as well as bad-guy types, that have access to the same encryption and software that we do. Some of the crackers have more tech than we do."

Stoddard knew Kelso used the correct term, crackers, instead of hackers. A lot of CIA agents still didn't know the difference, but the gulf between was worlds apart.

On-screen, Jackson Garrett, the man who had piloted the amphibious aircraft in the lightning raid on *Charity's Smile,* talked with the bartender. Three other monitors showed different views of the pilot. Stoddard had seeded the club with his own people.

"These guys still don't know we're in the neighborhood?" Stoddard asked.

"No." Kelso was quiet while he looked at the monitors. "We kept track of the places where the Moon Shadow triad's computer systems were violated. They're definitely interested in the British Columbian holdings."

"Play devil's advocate for me," Stoddard said. "Why would these people shift from tracking a nuclear device to Moon Shadow triad holdings in British Columbia?"

"Because they IDed the Zhao woman," Kelso said.

"And what are they going to do in Vancouver?"

"Find out more about the Moon Shadow triad."

"They could do that here," Stoddard pointed out. He watched the computer monitors relaying video feeds from the Vancouver bar. On-screen, Jackson Garrett left the bar.

"Hong Kong is too hot for them," Kelso said. "Also, the Moon Shadow organization is weak in Vancouver. Those people can be compromised. The Zhao woman is still concentrating on moving her legitimate businesses into Vancouver, not the illegal stuff. Eric Barnes is a throwback connection from her father's day."

Stoddard glanced at his watch. "Saengkeo Zhao should be in Los Angeles by now."

"She's been on the ground for two hours," Kelso said.

"What about Corbin?"

"She hasn't checked in."

"But she's in L.A.?"

Kelso hesitated. "We think so."

There were too many variables going on, and Stoddard knew it. Besides the missing nukes from *Kursk* that had been brokered through the Russian *mafiya,* the surprise team that had interrupted Saengkeo Zhao's recovery of the nuke from *Charity's Smile* and the trouble Saengkeo had stirred up in Hong Kong among the triads, there still remained the problem of Pei-Ling Bao to resolve.

As Jackson Garrett passed out of sight of the people inside the Nautilus Club, Stoddard tapped a key on the keyboard. The view on the center monitor shimmered, then took up the video feed of the security camera mounted on the wall outside the club. The setup wasn't as good as if he'd had a more direct satellite link, but Stoddard was used to working with what came to hand.

The pilot walked toward Eric Barnes.

"He's after Barnes," Kelso said. "Like we thought."

Stoddard nodded. "Give the order. Bring in this son of a bitch. I want to know who he is."

6

Vancouver, British Columbia

As he approached the hallway to the bathrooms in the Nautilus Club, Grimaldi took a small tube from his jacket. Crushing the tube between his forefinger and thumb broke the two thin plastic membranes inside the tube. When the two chemicals from the separate compartments mixed, the tube heated, proof that the chemicals had activated.

Stepping through the doorway to the left of the merman statue, Grimaldi looked down the hall outside the Nautilus Club and spotted Eric Barnes, Dobbins and the other two men standing in front of the elevators. Two cages lined the wall in front of them, mirrored by two more cages on the wall behind them.

"What was Barnes's last television appearance?" Grimaldi kept his voice low so no sound traveled. The boisterous noise from the Nautilus Club behind him echoed in the hallway.

Price answered at once, as he had known she would. "The Learning Channel. It was called *The Unseen Touch.* A special on set decorators. It aired three weeks ago, but the show was a rerun from two years ago."

Dobbins turned, staring at Grimaldi.

Without hesitation, the pilot raised his beer in a salute. "Hey, wait a minute."

Dobbins nodded to the two men with them. Both of them turned and intercepted Grimaldi, stopping him three feet short of Barnes.

"Hey," Grimaldi complained. "Relax. I just wanted an autograph."

"Get him out of here," Dobbins growled.

The two men started to walk Grimaldi backward.

Barnes regarded Grimaldi with a sardonic smile.

C'mon, guy, Grimaldi thought desperately. With an ego the size you gotta be carrying around, this has gotta flip your trigger.

"Stop," Barnes said, putting a hand out.

The two men halted, still holding Grimaldi but not being too gentle.

"Do you know me?" Barnes asked.

"Sure," Grimaldi said. "Eric Barnes. You worked on the *X-Files*. The bartender knows you, too. I was talking to her about you. I was going to see about an autograph, but you left the bar before I got up the nerve. I had to hurry like hell to catch up with you." He glanced at the two men holding him. "Look, I caught one of the shows you did for TLC. *The Unseen Touch.* I just wanted an autograph."

"From a props procurer?" Barnes asked.

"A props manager on *X-Files*," Grimaldi corrected. "You're not exactly your average props guy, are you?" The question was a dare, designed to touch Barnes's ego and get him out beyond the protection of his partner and bodyguards.

"No," Barnes agreed. "I'm not." He looked at the two men. "Let him go."

Reluctantly the two men stepped back.

Grimaldi straightened his jacket with his free hand, taking the opportunity to transfer his beer to the hand that held the tube. He walked toward Barnes and took a business card from his jacket pocket. "This is the best I have."

Barnes took the car and looked at it. "Jackson Garrett. You're a pilot? For Lucid Reality dotcom."

"Yeah. I'm up here with my boss."

"Seeing the sights?"

"As much as I can."

Taking the pen Dobbins offered, Barnes hastily scribbled on back of the business card. "I'm going to personalize this, Garrett. If it turns up on eBay, I'll know who put it there."

"I'm going to keep it," Grimaldi said. "Like I said, I was a big fan of the show."

Barnes handed back the card. Acting flustered, Grimaldi reached for the card with the hand that held the beer. He fumbled the beer. "Oops. Sorry." As he grabbed for the glass with both hands, he tagged the underside of Barnes's sleeve with the chemical tube.

Cursing, Barnes stepped back, barely avoiding the amber deluge that hit the carpet floor at his feet.

Moving swifter than his bulk would have led someone to believe, Dobbins fisted Grimaldi's jacket and shoved him backward against the wall. Dobbins had his hand at his belt-line under his jacket. No doubt remained in Grimaldi's head that the man held a weapon.

"Asshole," Dobbins growled.

"Sorry," Grimaldi said, palming the marker tube. He felt the heat of the chemicals brush across his fingertips as he put the tube in his pocket. The heated sensation was uncomfortable, but the chemicals' effects weren't caustic.

A group of people walked through the hallway, gazing uncomfortably toward Grimaldi and Dobbins. The pilot knew that if there hadn't been witnesses, Dobbins would have hit him. The file Price had turned up had indicated the man liked violence.

"Stay," Dobbins ordered.

Grimaldi made a show of looking mad but unwilling to do more than offer lip service. "Hey, man, you didn't have to put your hands on me. It was just a mistake. The glass slipped, that's all."

One of the elevator cages on the other side of the hallway opened. The black man put a foot inside the cage, blocking the door as three young women stepped off and headed toward the bar.

Barnes entered the elevator cage, flanked by the two body-guards. Dobbins leaned on his hand holding Grimaldi. The man held up a forefinger, looking down the finger like a gun-sight. "You done fucked up once tonight, flyboy. Cut your losses and stay the hell away from Mr. Barnes."

Grimaldi resisted the impulse to grab Dobbins's arm and break the elbow. He also resisted the temptation to dropkick the man in the crotch. Instead, he said nothing and tried to look afraid and angry at the same time.

Dobbins shoved his hand against Grimaldi's chest. The pilot went with the force instead of twisting away from it. The back of his head popped against the wall behind him.

Dobbins joined Barnes and the other two men in the ele-vator cage. A moment later, the elevator doors closed.

"Okay," Grimaldi gritted, "did you get it?" He knew the play-acting with Dobbins had been necessary, but tucking his tail between his legs was something he'd never been good at.

"We're live," Price replied. "The chemical marker is show-ing up five by five."

"Good," Grimaldi said. "Copy that, Striker?"

"Striker copies, Mustang," Bolan replied over the frequency.

Grimaldi stood in front of the elevators. Only a moment passed before the doors opened on one of the cages.

"Hold the elevator."

Surprised, Grimaldi turned and found Selena the bartender trotting toward him. Not knowing what to do, he placed a hand against the cage doors to keep them open and smiled uncertainly. "What are you doing?" he asked.

"I'm on break," Selena answered. "Thought I'd catch up to you and see what you were doing."

"Window-shopping," Grimaldi said. Without warning, the receiver-transceiver plugged into his ear filled with white noise. The sound wasn't loud enough to be painful, but the constant absence of hearing in the ear was disconcerting. "My boss called. Looks like I may be here for breakfast."

"So what are you shopping for? None of the shops are open at this time of night." Selena grinned. "Except for the Naughty 'n' Nice shop. They're not exactly Victoria's Secret, and most of the stuff you'd find there would make old Victoria blush. They specialize in latex, vinyl and gel, all battery operated and of impressive length."

Grimaldi's thoughts centered on Eric Barnes. Bolan was going to take the offensive, but Grimaldi had planned on being there to back him up.

"Actually," Grimaldi said, resisting the impulse to tap the ear transceiver in an effort to reactivate the device, "my boss was wanting me to look at some of that office space you were talking about."

"Then you'll want to see the sixth floor." Selena tapped the 6 key and stepped back. The elevator doors closed with a hum, shutting out the raucous noise of techno-trance music from the Nautilus Club. "And maybe we can take a tour of Naughty 'n' Nice on our way back down."

"Look," Grimaldi said, "I don't know how long your break is, but I could be looking at offices for a while. My boss is pretty picky about what he wants."

Without another word, Selena pushed herself into

Grimaldi's arms. Her hands slid under his jacket and roamed over his body while her lips found his in a heated rush.

"Ever done it in an elevator before?" Selena asked, disengaging from the kiss.

Grimaldi started to answer, but cold steel grazed his throat. The knife blade nicked the skin over his jugular just hard enough to bring warm blood that trickled down his neck.

"Just be still," Selena advised him. Her eyes had turned flat and hard, and her voice had dropped the sultry tones. The elevator cage rose up smoothly through the building. "Maybe you'll get to live."

LEANING FORWARD, keeping his weight evenly distributed to take on the recoil of the compressed-air cannon, Mack Bolan took aim at the building across Howe Street. The ugly, viciously barbed head of the spear jutted from the cannon's mouth. Neon lights glinted briefly against the razor-sharp edges that the black matte finish hadn't been able to quite blunt.

"Mustang is off-line," Price said.

"What happened?" Bolan slid his finger over the cannon's trigger.

"I don't know. He was met."

"By whom?"

"My guess is it's the woman bartender. The thermal imaging we're getting through the satellite feed looks female. We've got a piece of conversation that sounded like a woman's voice before Mustang's transmitter went down. There was only one woman that Mustang talked to in the target zone."

"Let me know if you get Mustang back with us," Bolan said.

"I will." Price was silent for a moment. "Your target is getting off at the fifth floor."

"I thought Mustang was told the target usually stayed on the sixth floor."

"He was. However, your target isn't following that pattern now."

The Executioner listened to the street noises and thought about Grimaldi. The wind rifled by him, colder than it had been and bringing more moisture. Rain was coming.

"We've got your target, Striker," Price said. "He's on your side of the building. Third office from the left as you view the structure."

Quietly the Executioner shifted the CO_2 cannon and took aim at the expanse of brick wall above the third office window. A light went on inside, throwing a golden cast over the window. "What's the setup inside?"

"Just like we discussed earlier," the mission controller said. "Outer and inner office. They're in the outer office now."

Bolan squeezed the cannon's trigger. The air cannon bucked against his shoulder with enough force to send twinges through his bruised chest.

The barbed spear leaped across the intervening distance above the street. High-pitched keening whirred as the cable paid out from the cannon's reel. Sparks flashed as the metal spear dug into the building's stone surface.

Moving quickly, Bolan anchored the cable to the HVAC unit squatting atop the roof. When the line was tight and secure, he reached into the equipment bag sitting at his feet and took out a mountain-climbing pulley. He clamped the pulley onto the cable and threw himself out over the street. Stretched tight as Bolan could by hand, the cable sagged a little, but held the downgrade angle he'd chosen for his attack.

The pulley whirred across the cable, barely audible above the voices from the people wandering the sidewalks and the cars filling the streets. Bolan held on, his body loose and ready beneath the cable. He kept his eyes focused on the lighted windows of the building in front of him.

"Striker," Price called, "we've confirmed that Mustang's signal is being jammed by a white-noise generator."

"Do you still have a lock on him?" the soldier asked.

"Affirmative. Besides the communications device, we've also got some of the targeting chemical he used to mark your target."

The pulley slid across the cable, quickly closing the gap. Bolan raised his feet and landed against the building's side only inches from one of the windows. The moon and clouds showed in the reflection. He used a D-ring clip to anchor himself to the pulley, then reached into his combat vest. Taking out a diamond-tipped glass cutter and a suction cup, he slapped the cup to the window and noticed the silvery glimmer around the edges. Closer inspection revealed that the silvery glimmer was alarm tape.

"Stony Base," Bolan called.

"Go," Price replied.

"I'm looking at an alarm system."

"There wasn't one in the building specs."

"It's here," Bolan assured her.

"Hold on."

Bolan had no choice. He pulled himself more tightly against the wall and braced his toes between a line of bricks to take some of the weight off the combat harness. He leaned close to the window and peered through the crack between the window's edge and the machine-driven blinds.

A small light illuminated the office inside. A large, ornate desk occupied the spot in front of the window, fronted by two leather chairs flanked by a couch on one side and an entertainment system and wet bar on the other. Movie and TV posters hung on the walls, all of them projects that Eric Barnes had been involved with.

The office looked exactly the way intel from Stony Man Farm had suggested it would. Only the shiny silver tape running around the inside of the window was new. Evidently someone had decided to upgrade the alarm systems. Bolan wondered if the decision had come from Eric Barnes or from Saengkeo Zhao after everything that had happened in Hong Kong. Perhaps it was even somehow tied in with her brother's murder only a short time ago.

And if the upgrade was tied into Syn-Tek Zhao's death, that meant it was probably also tied up in the missing nuclear weapons from the downed Russian submarine, *Kursk*. U.S. Navy special forces teams had recovered the one from *Charity's Smile*, which Bolan had liberated from the Russian *mafiya*.

"We found the alarm system," Price said a moment later. "There's a backup system logged into the telephone grid. If the contacts are broken, three messages go out. The first one is internal to another office on the sixth floor."

"Home security," Bolan said. "Barnes doesn't want anyone outside looking into his business."

"Yes. The other two signals flow through the communications switchboard two minutes after the first one."

Bolan took that in, knowing the two minutes were for the security teams on-site to assess and handle the damage if it could be done. Or to get rid of any incriminating evidence if possible.

"The other two signals go to a security monitoring system, and to the Vancouver PD," Price went on. "However, as of this moment, breaking those contacts will trigger none of those events."

"What about Mustang?" Bolan inscribed a large circle on the glass.

"He's still being moved through the sixth floor. Two more people have joined them."

"Audio pickup hasn't been restored?"

"No."

Bolan clamped down on the anxiety that trickled through

him. Whatever trouble Grimaldi was in, they were both dead if he didn't maintain his focus. He completed the circle in the glass, then grabbed the suction cup and prepared to pop the piece free.

The door to the office swept open suddenly, and Bolan stayed his hand. He peered through the space between the blinds and the window frame. The harsh light tore into his right eye.

Two hardcases, a white man and a black man, entered first. Then Harvey Dobbins, looking very much like the picture Price had sent along with the intel package from Stony Man Farm, strode into the room. The fingers of his right hand were knotted in the hair of a young Asian woman.

Steel manacles bound the woman's hands behind her, and gray duct tape covered her mouth. She looked to be in her early twenties. Fear made her eyes unnaturally wide. She wore Capri jeans and a see-through white gauze long-sleeved shirt over a midnight-blue halter. Red tinted the ends of her short-cropped black hair. Rolled calf-high boots with stiletto heels caught at the thick carpet.

Dobbins yanked the woman forward by her hair. The tape muted the woman's pain-filled bleat. Her stiletto heels dug into the carpet and tripped her. Dobbins let her go sprawling. One sleeve of the gauze shirt ripped from her shoulder on impact and left her upper arm bare.

Eric Barnes stepped into the doorway.

The woman flopped over on her back and used her feet and elbows to crawl away from the man.

Barnes smiled at her, but the facial expression was cold and cruel. He crossed the room, stepping through the space the woman had vacated.

The woman kept backing until she reached one of the leather chairs in front of the big desk. She hit her head and stopped, chest rising and falling quickly like a trapped animal's.

"Who is she?" Barnes demanded as he sat on the corner of the big desk.

Dobbins snapped his fingers. The white man accompanying the ex-cop produced a small black handbag. Dobbins took the handbag, then tossed it to Barnes. "De-Ying Wu. Her friends call her DeeDee."

Barnes upended the handbag across the immaculate desktop, scattering articles over the blotter. "And should I know De-Ying Wu?"

The woman stared at her captors.

"I got the name, Striker," Price said over the headset. "We're running it down now."

Bolan watched, trying to get a read on the body language of the men inside the room. The big man was constantly aware of the numbers on the play ticking through his mind.

The Executioner unsnapped the restraining strap holding the .44 Magnum Desert Eagle in counterterrorist drop leather on his right knee. He flicked off the safety, holding himself parallel to the building with his weight on his legs.

Barnes sorted through the debris on the desk. He found a plastic rectangle and plucked it from the other contents. His eyes scanned the information on the card, then cut to Dobbins.

"De-Ying Wu. Private investigator. Licensed by Washington State in the United States," Barnes said. "Is this real?"

Dobbins nodded. "One hundred percent bona fide."

"Who's she working for?"

"The same people you work for."

Barnes gazed back at the woman. "Is that the truth, DeeDee? Are you here working for the Zhao triad?"

Wu tried to speak, but the tape over her mouth made her incomprehensible.

"Striker," Price said, "the information checks out. There is a De-Ying Wu licensed in Redmond, Washington. We're accessing more information now."

Barnes leaned over Wu, his fingers closing over one end of the tape. He pulled experimentally, tugging at her flesh, as well, without stripping the tape away.

"When I take this tape off your mouth," Barnes said, "you're not going to scream, right?"

Wu shook her head.

"Good," Barnes went on. "Because if you scream, I'm going to get pissed." He yanked the tape away.

Wu screamed, then ducked back immediately as if to escape a blow.

Barnes regarded the woman with idle speculation, watching her as she screamed. A mocking smile played on his lips.

Wu continued screaming until she had no breath left. None of the men inside the room made an effort to stop her.

"Go ahead and scream, bitch," Barnes said. "The fucking room is soundproof. Why do you think you were brought here?"

Panic filled Wu as she gasped for air and looked around the room. She got her feet under her and struggled into a standing position. Before she got her balance, Barnes surged forward and backhanded her, knocking her reeling onto the couch. Blood dribbled down her chin from the corner of her mouth. She screamed again.

"You're going to tell me what you know, bitch," Barnes said. "I want to know who hired you."

"Saengkeo Zhao," Wu said. "Dobbins already told you that."

Barnes stood before her, showing every inclination of striking her again.

Bolan held his ground. If De-Ying Wu was a private investigator working for Saengkeo Zhao, the woman wasn't exactly an innocent. But if someone had taken Grimaldi, the Executioner had to wonder why the pilot hadn't been brought to the soundproof room, as well.

"What about Mustang?" Bolan whispered as he watched the people inside the room.

"Mustang is stationary," Price responded. "Sixth floor. Two people have joined them. We're hacking into Wu's banking records. If there's a tie to any of the business interests in the subject we've been tracking, we'll find it."

"Why did Zhao hire you?" Barnes demanded.

"She thought you were skimming from the profits," Wu said. "And she thought you had betrayed her."

Barnes looked amused. "And what did you find out?"

Pure vehemence filled Wu's pretty face. "I think she has every right to think you'd betray her. You don't have a very good reputation out on the street, Barnes."

"On the contrary," Barnes retorted. "I have an excellent reputation. I have connections all over this part of the world. That's why Syn-Tek Zhao hired me to handle operations in Vancouver for him."

"Fine," Wu said. "We disagree on a couple small points. It's no big deal." She tried to come across as brave, but Bolan spotted the cracks in the facade and knew that the woman was terrified.

Barnes turned his attention to Dobbins. "Where did you find her?"

"Backtracking you through the customs house."

"And what was she doing there?"

"Checking on shipments," Dobbins said.

"Drug shipments probably," Price supplied over the headset. "The Vancouver PD hasn't been able to crack Barnes's supply-and-distribution routes yet. He's just a whisper in the overall tide of heroin coming into British Columbia. No one has been able to pin anything on him."

Bolan knew that. The lack of information regarding Eric Barnes and the man's affiliation with the Moon Shadow triad was the biggest reason the Executioner had targeted the man.

Bolan wanted Zhao to know that he was stalking her on her most prized turf. The Moon Shadow triad was funneling a lot of its money into the British Columbia developments.

"*My* shipments?" Barnes asked.

"Yeah," Dobbins said. "She was also trying to buy off information about your bank records here and in the off-shore accounts down in the Caymans."

Barnes looked back at Wu. "Why were you doing that?"

"Because Saengkeo Zhao doesn't trust you the way her brother did," Wu said defiantly. "And if anything happens to me, she's going to come looking for you."

"Is that true?" Barnes asked Dobbins.

Dobbins shrugged. "Maybe. But Wu also has an ex-husband who could look real good for her murder."

"Where is he?"

Dobbins grinned. "We have him. Guys I put on him in Seattle snatched him yesterday. He's here in Vancouver."

"Why would he look good for her murder?" Barnes asked.

"Because the son of a bitch is a sick fuck," Dobbins said. "Wu's already had to file a restraining order against him after the divorce. He put her in the hospital twice so far, and one of those times included a weeklong stay in the intensive-care unit. He broke her jaw. They had to wire her mouth shut, and she ate through an IV and a straw for a month."

Wu's resolve shattered. Desperation filled her eyes.

"Good," Barnes commented. "Then we'll make it look like the ex followed this bitch up here and took her out."

"We can tie him to an alias one of my guys used to fly up here the day we took the ex down." Dobbins shrugged. "I'd have killed this bitch myself, except I knew that you enjoyed the work."

"I do," Barnes agreed. Looking around for a moment, he leaned down and plucked the plastic liner from the trash can at the side of the desk. He dumped a handful of litter onto the carpet and looked at De-Ying Wu as he opened the plastic liner in both hands. "Hold her."

Bolan considered his options as Dobbins and the white man grabbed the bound woman by the arms and pinned her in a sitting position against the floor. She screamed and shook her head, trying in vain to dodge Barnes and the plastic liner. When the liner slipped over her head, the screams muted and her breath fogged the liner.

"Keep the lock on Mustang," Bolan said as he kicked against the wall. "I'm going after him next." The pulley spun fluidly back up the grade of the cable. Five feet out from the building, gravity took over again. The Executioner unsnapped the D-ring and hung on to the pulley with one hand, suspended over the five-story drop to the front of the building below.

Even as he started sliding back toward the building, Bolan lifted the Desert Eagle and squeezed the trigger three times. The big semiautomatic pistol bucked against his palm, and the .44-caliber Magnum boattails slammed against the broad expanse of the window.

Glass shattered, then came down in shards.

Bolan's combat senses flared, slowing time until he could see the individual pieces spinning and catching moonlight. The blinds jerked, then tore from their moorings, collapsing in a wave of plastic and glass. The soldier leaned forward, pushing off the pulley toward the window.

7

Whipping his left arm forward, Bolan raked at the falling blinds and managed to propel himself forward. He landed in a crouch inside the room behind and to one side of the big desk. His heartbeat echoed in his ears, distorted by the adrenaline that pumped him up to maximum velocity. He'd fired three shots from the Desert Eagle, leaving four in the magazine and a live round under the hammer.

Startled, Barnes roped an arm under De-Ying Wu's chin and yanked her from the carpet. He held her in front of him as a shield.

Dobbins extended his right arm, and a Semmerling .45 ACP derringer jumped into his waiting hand. His finger fell across the trigger immediately because the weapon had no trigger guard. The barrel spit flame and the crescendo of thunder filled the office space.

Still wreathed in the loose blinds, the Executioner threw himself to the left, sweeping his left arm across his body and clearing the tangled plastic slats. He brought up the heavy .44 Magnum pistol and squeezed off two rounds. Thunder rolled through the room on the heels of the first detonations.

Both boattail slugs caught Dobbins in the chest and punched him backward into the white man who had accompanied him. They went down in a tangle of arms and legs.

The black man ripped an Uzi from a shoulder drop rig. The machine pistol stuttered to life before the barrel even came level. A staggered line of bullets chopped into the carpet and climbed the desk. Another salvo ripped across the desktop, blasting through the computer monitor, keyboard, Wu's purse and the phone. Wooden splinters, chunks of rubber and pieces of plastic danced in the air. The monitor spilled its guts in a rush of electrical smoke.

Still moving to the left, the Executioner unleathered his Beretta 93-R. He drew the pistol in his left hand and slid his left wrist under his right wrist as he exhausted running room and smacked against the wall. Supporting his right hand with his left, he fired his three remaining shots from the Eagle at the Uzi wielder's head.

One of the bullets missed entirely, gouging a hole in the wall behind the gunner. The second round smacked into the side of the man's head and tore his right ear away in a rush of crimson. The third round punched a hole in the center of the man's face, snapping his head back.

The Desert Eagle's slide blew back empty as the last brass cartridge ejected. Aware of the man's movement underneath Dobbins, the Executioner shifted the Beretta to him as the man pointed a 9 mm Glock and pulled the trigger.

Four rounds buzzed by Bolan's head and hammered the wall beside him, missing him by mere inches.

The Executioner leveled the 93-R and stroked the trigger twice. The Beretta carried subsonic 9 mm rounds that probably wouldn't penetrate Dobbins's corpse. Both shots Bolan fired hammered the man, ripping into his throat and into his face.

The man dropped his weapon, dead before his hand hit the floor.

Still braced against the wall, Bolan stared at Eric Barnes and De-Ying Wu over the 93-R's barrel. A slight gunpowder stink scorched the air.

Fear tightened Barnes's features. "Who are you?"

De-Ying Wu stood on her toes, barely shielding the bigger man who held her. The plastic liner covered her head and looked like a bubble-shaped astronaut's helmet from an old science-fiction movie, except for the fact that she was struggling to breathe in and only succeeded in sucking the plastic into her nostrils.

"Let the woman go," Bolan said in a graveyard voice.

"If I do," Barnes replied, "you'll kill me. You didn't have a problem killing the others."

Bolan held his stance but dropped his right hand, leathering the Desert Eagle. He heard the soft whisper of the numbers falling on the play, knowing that Grimaldi was up to his ass in alligators elsewhere in the building. He kept the Beretta trained on Barnes.

Wu struggled weakly, gasping against the plastic that covered her face.

Barnes tightened his grip, manhandling the woman with ease. "Time's running out for you," he taunted. "You keep waiting on how to decide to handle this situation, she's going to asphyxiate."

"You die the second after she does," Bolan promised.

"Then we'll have to work something out." Barnes took a step back toward the office door. He kept his forearm locked under the woman's throat.

"Striker," Price said over the headset, "Mustang is in motion on the floor above you. And four men are running through the hallway approaching the office."

"Who are they?" Bolan asked.

"We don't know."

Barnes glanced around nervously as he kept creeping toward the door. "You got somebody watching us?"

Bolan said nothing, waiting for the man to give him an opening. If possible, he needed to keep Barnes alive. Barnes knew a lot about the Moon Shadow triad's operation in Vancouver.

The soldier took a step after Barnes.

Barnes halted and twisted Wu's head. The woman yelped in pain, barely able to make a sound inside the plastic bag with so little air remaining to her. She raised her foot and stamped at Barnes's foot, but he easily evaded her.

"Move again," Barnes threatened Bolan, "and I break her pretty little neck."

Bolan stopped.

"The four men are in the outer office," Price informed Bolan.

"Mr. Barnes," someone said.

"In here," Barnes snarled. "One guy. He killed Dobbins and the others. Take him down." He set himself and tried to drag the woman after him.

Knowing he'd run out of time and alternatives, Bolan squeezed off a single bullet. The 9 mm round cut through the air, making only a discreet *chuff* that was hardly audible over Barnes's voice.

The hollowpoint round caught Barnes in the ear and ripped through the other side in an explosion of blood and bone. Crimson droplets slapped against Wu's see-through gauze blouse and the plastic bag over her head. She turned and tried to scream, succeeding in ripping her lips free of the tape. The sound was startlingly loud because the bullet had come close enough to her face to rip through the plastic.

As Barnes fell dead, Bolan launched into motion, crossing the room in four long strides. He caught the front of the woman's blouse and yanked her forward. He felt the thin fabric tear and hoped that the garment stayed together long enough to enable him to save the woman. As she cleared the doorway and Barnes's corpse dropped to the floor in the next room, Bolan slipped his hip against the open door inside the inner office.

The four men were all hardcases dressed in casual street wear. Sound suppressors elongated the barrels of their pistols, immediately marking them as something other than undercover or off-duty police officers or legitimate security guards.

Bolan slammed the door shut with his hip and let go of the woman. He locked the door only a heartbeat before bullets punched through the panels. Splinters tumbled through the air as he reached the woman and ripped the suffocating bag from her head.

"Who...are...you?" she gasped.

"The guy who is going to get you out of here if I can." Bolan leathered the Beretta and changed out magazines in the Desert Eagle. So far, the men hadn't tried to rush the door, but bullets tore through the thin wood and the wall.

The woman lay on her side. Her eyes showed white and her breath came in pants. "Dobbins. He had...a key...for the...cuffs." She raised her arms behind her back to show the steel encircling her wrists.

Bolan stayed low, resting on one knee, the Desert Eagle in his right hand while he searched Dobbins's clothing.

"The four men are holding their positions outside the doorway, Striker," Price relayed.

"Understood," Bolan replied.

"The police have been alerted," the mission controller went on. "They're en route."

"What about Mustang?" Bolan found the handcuff key by itself in Dobbins's shirt pocket.

"Still on the sixth floor and moving."

"Have you IDed his captors?"

"Not yet."

"No communications between Barnes and that group?"

"None that we've detected," Price admitted.

"There would have been communications," Bolan said as he duckwalked over to De-Ying Wu, "if they were with Barnes."

"I agree."

"So the people who snatched Mustang are part of another group." Bolan opened the cuff holding the woman's right wrist.

"I think so, too," Price said. "Someone else who has been watching Barnes."

"I need them IDed," Bolan pointed out.

"We're working on it."

Wu rubbed her bruised wrist. The cuffs dangled from her left wrist. "Who are you talking to?"

"The Blue Fairy." Bolan pressed the handcuff key into her hand. "We need to move."

Wu bent to the task of removing the cuffs.

Remaining low, aware that the gunfire from the outer office had stopped, Bolan reached into his combat vest and took out a small chunk of C-4 plastic explosive. The C-4 was small and had been equipped with a signal detonator. He'd planned to use the explosive primarily as a distraction.

The soldier slapped the C-4 to the frame beside the door and activated the detonator.

"Striker, those men are advancing in the outer office," Price said.

Bolan stood and aimed the Desert Eagle at the door. He fired through the entire magazine, sending spinning brass ricocheting across the room. Fist-sized holes appeared in the door.

"One man down," Price said.

Bolan spun, shucking the empty magazine and sliding another into place. He leathered the pistol and reached for Wu.

The woman moved with lightning speed, shoving the Glock pistol that had been dropped earlier into Bolan's face.

Reacting immediately, the soldier slapped the weapon from the woman's hands as a fresh wave of gunfire from the outer room exploded through the door. Bolan grabbed Wu's upper arm and yanked her upright.

"Move," the Executioner growled.

"Who are you?"

"For now," Bolan suggested, "I'm a friend. And if you don't get out of here, you're dead." He shoved her toward the window.

"You came here after me?"

"No." Bolan took an electronic detonator from his combat vest. The detonator came attached to an elastic band that he slipped over his fingers so that the device nestled against his palm.

Gunfire rattled through the door again. Bullets smashed through the thin plasterboard and the window glass behind the desk. A mournful tug horn blasted out in Burrard Inlet. The gathering storm chose that moment to unleash the pending fury. Great sheets of rain washed down over the city.

Wu glanced out the broken window. The wind shoved her red-dyed hair into wilder disarray. "We're not jumping," she said.

"No, we're not," Bolan replied. He stepped in beside her, keeping his body against hers so if she made a move to get another weapon he'd know. "You've got to trust me."

"Trust you? Mister, I don't even know who the hell you are."

"I'm the guy who saved your life," Bolan replied.

Another hail of bullets knocked chunks from the door.

"At least," he amended, "I've saved your life so far." He

leaned out the window, drew the Beretta and fired a triburst at the sixth-floor window above them. Then he dodged back inside the office, barely avoiding the rain of glass shards that tumbled down and reflected the neon lights coming from below. A canvas canopy along the sidewalk businesses kept the deadly glass from striking the street or any pedestrians.

"Let me guess," Wu said. "We're going up."

"Got it in one," Bolan assured her, leathering the Beretta.

Wu glanced at the side of the building with obvious doubt. "Do you realize how dangerous that is?"

The silence from the guns in the outer office spoke volumes, and Bolan knew the woman was aware of it. "We can't stay here."

"How do you plan on getting up there?"

Bolan reached into a thigh pocket and produced a collapsible minigrappling hook. He twisted the hook and the prongs popped out. The line tied to the hook was only twenty feet long, knotted every eighteen inches. He leaned out the window and flipped the grappling hook over the next window ledge.

"Can you climb?" Bolan asked.

"Yes."

"Do it."

The woman hesitated a moment, but the silence in the room was splintered by police sirens in the distance. She stepped up onto the ledge and swiftly climbed the rope, bracing her legs against the wall. Her stiletto heels caught between the bricks.

"Hold on." Bolan caught one of the boots and yanked it off. He let it drop to the canopy below.

"Hey," Wu protested, "do you know how many Gucci dollars, American, that you just tossed away in such a cavalier manner?"

Bolan was more surprised that the woman was calm

enough to even think to protest. He seized her other boot and tossed it, as well. "Go."

Wu cursed and bent to the task of scaling the wall with greater ease.

"Stony Base," Bolan said.

"Go," Price replied.

"Can you guide me through the office above?"

"That's affirmative, Striker. We've got the blueprints on the buildings. We're tracking Mustang now."

Bolan stepped out onto the ledge as Wu pulled herself into the window above. With his weight on the line, the grappling hook would be harder to dislodge, and he didn't trust the woman not to try to rid herself of him. He swarmed up the line, feeling the bruised muscles in his chest ache from the exertion.

"Striker," Price said, "be advised that the three men have broken through the doorway to the inner office."

Bolan reached up and caught the next window ledge. As he did, he pressed the detonator button.

The explosion in the office below vibrated through the building. A body wreathed in flames hurtled through the window, then dropped like a comet to the canopy below.

Bolan watched as the dead man landed in the middle of the spread canvas and nearly tore the awning from its moorings. Then he pulled himself up into the next office.

Darkness filled the room. The Executioner changed magazines in the 93-R, then glanced at the woman standing barely revealed in the shadows.

"Stay or go," Bolan said. "I've got a friend up here to find."

The woman hesitated only a moment. "Stay," she said. "Barnes has more men in the building."

Bolan nodded. "Try to stay out of the way."

De-Ying Wu, private investigator, shot him a rueful look. "Thanks for the overwhelming vote of confidence."

The Executioner took point, moving swiftly through the office door into the hallway beyond.

SOUND CONTINUED to explode in Jack Grimaldi's head with dizzying intensity. He felt certain that Selena and the two men with her were responsible for the failure of the radio transceiver and the resulting backlash of noise. If they were, they had to know what the transceiver was doing to him. However, they probably also knew that the noise was keeping him disoriented.

Selena had changed the knife she'd held Grimaldi captive with for a small Beretta .380 semiautomatic pistol. Maybe the pistol didn't have the sheer knockdown power of its bigger brothers, but it was just as lethal.

The two men who had joined the woman displayed a totally professional behavior. They'd locked Grimaldi's hands behind his back with disposable plastic cuffs without a word when Selena had guided him from the elevator, then had taken charge of him.

The hallway through the heart of the sixth floor was well lighted. Neon signs glowed in the spacious windows of shops.

Grimaldi felt a little hope then that someone might see him and call for a cop. Of course, that might have caused even more problems, but the pilot had the distinct feeling that dealing with law-enforcement questions would be a lot better than dealing with Selena and her two friends.

The lady bartender took the lead and stopped at the first door on the left. They were short of the concourse area proper, just back of the circle of soft light blushing out from the shops.

The pain drilled into Grimaldi's head with a pounding physical presence. Nausea swamped his stomach and turned his legs weak. He had trouble focusing his eyes. The Maintenance sign showed up in double vision, and he had to read the letters three times before the word made any sense.

One of the men stepped forward with lock picks. He worked the lock for just an instant, then the door opened. The room beyond was dark until Selena swept an arm on the wall inside. Fluorescent lights snapped on with a soft white glow.

Selena spoke, but Grimaldi couldn't hear her. She pointed to the center of the room. A furnace and janitorial equipment occupied the back half of the room. Cabinets on either side of the room held paper and linen supplies, and cleaners and solutions in gallon jugs.

One of the men closed the maintenance-room door behind them.

Selena took a small, folding step stool from beside a small mop closet that contained a mop bucket. She opened the stool in the center of the room and stepped away.

The two men holding Grimaldi's arms yanked him down onto the top step of the two-step platform. The restraining bar at the back slammed across his kidneys with bruising force. One of the men knelt and secured another loop of plastic cuffs around Grimaldi's ankles. He cinched the plastic restraining strap so tight that the blood flow was cut off and Grimaldi began to lose feeling at once.

You're about to be in a world of hurt, Jack, Grimaldi thought. He blinked and tried to clear his vision, but the sound throbbing through his skull made it impossible to focus for more than a second or two at a time, and somehow made him light sensitive to even the fluorescence.

The two men stepped backward and drew sound-suppressed .40-caliber pistols.

Selena kept her .380 clutched in her fist. A small smile flirted with her lips. The expression was cold and cruel, and somehow seemed more natural than the come-on looks she'd been giving Grimaldi in the Nautilus Club. She stepped forward, staying out of the line of fire of her two companions.

Professional, Grimaldi realized. He tried to gather his scattered thoughts, tried to remember if he'd detected any hint of an accent that had been in the exchange they'd had. But there was nothing. Her speech had been as flat and uninflected as a CNN TV newscaster's.

The woman hooked a finger into Grimaldi's ear and dug out the earplug transceiver.

The roar of noise in Grimaldi's head died away, but the loss of the constant sound was almost as disorienting as its presence had been.

Selena dropped the transceiver on the floor and crushed the device underfoot. Tiny pieces of silicon gleamed in the light.

"Is there anything else?" she demanded.

Her voice sounded hollow and distant to Grimaldi. He tried to sit up straighter, taking stock of what kind of shape he was in. His sense of balance was still affected, and he felt uncertain. Even if he hadn't been bound hand and foot, he didn't think he'd have been able to put up much of a fight.

One of the men took a small device that looked like a PDA from his jacket pocket. Both of them wore casual wear, sports shirts over jeans and corduroy respectively. Both had short haircuts and healthy tans, like guys who spent their days on golf courses and their nights helping out the PTA.

The man waved the device over Grimaldi, tracking slowly from his head to his feet.

"Nothing," the man said, placing the device back into his pocket.

"No GPS locater sewn into his jacket or clothing?" Selena asked.

"Nothing," the man repeated flatly. He glanced at his watch. "We don't have a lot of time here. If Control is correct about these guys—"

"Control is," Selena said.

"Then the shitstorm is due to start at any minute," the man

went on. "From what we've been told, these jokers don't waste time."

Selena gazed at Grimaldi in open speculation. "Is that right, flyboy? Is there about to be a shitstorm?"

"I don't know what you're talking abou—"

The woman swept her gun hand across Grimaldi's face with startling speed. The .380's barrel hurt like hell, and the front blade of the gunsight slashed into the pilot's cheek.

Grimaldi didn't try to hold back a cry of pain. If anything, maybe someone outside the door would hear him and call someone to investigate.

Selena reached out with her free hand and caught Grimaldi's chin. She brought him back around to face her.

His cheek throbbed, swelling visibly by heartbeats.

"Don't talk like I'm an idiot," Selena advised in a cold, controlled voice. "This is state-of-the-art communications equipment." She nudged the pieces of the transceiver scattered across the floor with the toe of her shoe. "Where did you get it?"

"The guy I'm working for," Grimaldi answered.

"Who are you working for?"

"I don't know." Even though he was expecting the blow, Grimaldi wasn't able to turn his head quickly enough to avoid any of the sudden impact. The pistol slammed against his face again. He felt his cheek split inside his mouth and tasted coppery blood. For a moment he thought he was going to pass out, but he hung on to the pain like a man gripping a life preserver.

"Wrong answer," Selena told Grimaldi. If there was any reticence in the woman about the violence she was using, she didn't show it.

Grimaldi faced her. He layered the hammering pain from his face into his consciousness, using the agony to sharpen his mind. After the audio assault from the transceiver, his brain felt like tapioca.

"I don't know who hired me," Grimaldi insisted. "I answered an ad. A blind-drop mailbox. Guy promised me money to do a job for him. Gave me half up front. And the transceiver you broke."

"You don't know who hired you?"

"Sometimes it's better if you don't know," the pilot replied. "Sometimes the people who hire you don't like anyone hanging around later who knows their business. Sometimes you end up getting whacked-out for learning more than any of you planned on you learning."

Selena glanced at one of the men. The guy shrugged. Behind them, the other man was opening a small, compact briefcase on a worktable.

Turning her attention back to Grimaldi, Selena said, "You're not as smart as you think you are."

"Lady," Grimaldi replied, "I don't think I'm as smart as you think I am."

The smile that touched Selena's mouth and eyes then seemed genuine.

The man with the briefcase reached in and brought out a notebook computer and a cell phone. He tapped a button, and the notebook computer monitor's LCD screen flickered and came to life.

"What were you supposed to do here?" Selena asked.

Grimaldi didn't try to lie. He hadn't picked up on Selena's two playmates. Probably if she'd made him, they'd been watching him; they would have seen the encounter with Barnes and his people in the hallway.

"I was supposed to let the guy who hired me know Eric Barnes was here," Grimaldi answered.

"Did you?"

"Yes."

The man with the notebook computer hooked a wire into the cell phone and touched the keypad. The monitor screen cleared instantly, bringing up an Internet connection. Since there was no buzz and whine of a modem connection, Grimaldi knew they'd been set up for a wireless DSL connection. And that meant there was a base camp somewhere within the building that wasn't far away.

Grimaldi's brain raced. There had been no communication with Barnes that he had seen. If his transceiver wasn't working, he was willing to bet that Selena and the two men hadn't been able to contact anyone, either.

They worked for someone else. But who remained to be seen.

"After you'd seen Barnes," Selena said, "what were you supposed to do."

"Follow him."

"Why?"

"I don't know." Grimaldi readied himself to be bashed again.

"We were told you had a partner."

"Yeah." Grimaldi saw no reason to lie about that. As professional as Selena and her crew were, they wouldn't have believed he'd come to the Nautilus Club without backup other than the transceiver.

"Where is he?"

"Outside."

"Where outside?"

"A van," Grimaldi answered. "About a block away."

"Was he in the communications loop?"

"Yeah."

"Then he knows you were taken," Selena stated.

Grimaldi didn't answer. He knew the woman didn't expect him to.

"What do you think your partner will do?" the woman asked.

Grimaldi hesitated. During his long association with Mack

Bolan, the pilot had been immersed in dangerous situations. Signing on with Stony Man Farm had increased the frequency of those situations, and upped the probability that he wouldn't make it back out of them alive. Grimaldi had accepted that the work he did would probably eventually get him killed, but he'd always figured that he'd go down piloting a plane or a jet or a helicopter for the Executioner or one of the Stony Man teams.

Not in a maintenance room.

"What do you think your partner will do?" Selena repeated with more force.

"Whatever he can," Grimaldi said.

The man at the notebook computer spoke up. "We've got him."

Who was we? Grimaldi wondered.

"Where is he?" Selena asked.

"One of the offices Barnes uses," the man said. "On the fifth floor."

Selena approached the notebook computer and stared at the screen. From the angle where he sat, Grimaldi couldn't see any of the images.

"He's trapped," Selena commented. "He'll never make it out of that room before Barnes's people kill him."

"Yeah, well, it's a little late for Barnes, isn't it?" the computer man asked. "Don't count this guy out." He tapped the screen. "See?"

"Do we have access to any security cameras outside the building?" Selena asked.

Grimaldi worked his cuffs but couldn't gain any leverage or looseness. The disposable bonds didn't allow any room once they were locked down until they were cut off.

"All the security cameras outside the building cover the rooftop and the street level," the man at the computer said.

"Then we don't know where he is," Selena said.

"Not until he hits the roof or the street."

"Dammit." Selena returned her attention to Grimaldi. "Will he come after you?"

"No," Grimaldi said. "He doesn't know where I am."

"What about the person who hired you?"

"Come on, lady," Grimaldi growled. "I'm a hired snoop. The person who hired me doesn't give a shit about me." But the pilot knew that if possible, Bolan would be there. He nodded toward the fragments of the transceiver strewed across the floor. "And you pretty much ended any chance of him knowing where I am."

"Call Control," Selena said. "Find out what we're supposed to do."

The man at the computer tapped the keys in quick syncopation.

An explosion shook the building, sounding not far away.

"What the hell was that?" Selena demanded.

"The flyboy's partner," the man at the computer said. "He just blew up the office and took out a handful of Barnes's hired muscle." He glanced up from the computer screen. "Control says to get this guy's fingerprints to run through AFIS, then dispose of him."

Grimaldi stared at the three people. He had no doubts of what the disposal involved.

Selena leveled the .380 at Grimaldi. "He doesn't have to be alive for us to scan his prints in."

8

Los Angeles, California

Saengkeo Zhao strode through the south concourse of the Tom Bradley International Terminal at LAX. The China Eastern flight from Kowloon had arrived eight minutes ahead of schedule, then burned twelve minutes while waiting to disembark. Even at the late-evening hour, the terminal was busy. Los Angeles was an international hub, a twenty-four-hour city that burned energy.

She wore lace-up jeans and a white camisole-type halter that smoothed and enhanced the curves hidden beneath the supple sand-colored leather jacket. She stood five feet six inches tall, which was enhanced by the heels on the Italian roll-top boots. Her black hair was cut squared off with her chin. Oakley sunglasses masked her eyes. A gold choker lay against the burnished caramel skin at her throat.

In her present clothing, Saengkeo knew she'd be taken for an American movie star or a wanna-be poseur at least ten years younger than she actually was. Perhaps even as young as twenty. She didn't look like the head of a Chinese crime cartel with international scope. One of the passengers aboard the flight had confused her with Tia Carrere. Either mistaken impression was fine; a proper mask for the L.A. scene. Even so, she felt naked without a pistol snugged under shoulder leather.

She passed a bookstore. A quick glance at the reflections in the shop's windows revealed no one following her with extraordinary interest. Of course, the people that were really good at trailing others wouldn't be immediately apparent.

Memories banged at the back of Saengkeo's mind. A few years ago, Syn-Tek had accompanied her to L.A. while their father had still been the head of the Moon Shadows. Syn-Tek had been given the benefit of an international education, as she had, but he'd never chosen to stray far from Hong Kong and mainland China. Her brother's interests had been like those of their father: primarily Eastern.

The gut-wrenching ache filled Saengkeo again for a moment. The pain of her brother's death had yet to abate. Ea-Han, the old man who had raised her like a grandfather, had told her she needed to grieve. But there hadn't been much time for grieving. She'd had to take over as head of her family's triad, and she had to continue the work her grandfather, father and brother had been doing to move the family business out of crime and into legitimate pursuits.

She missed Syn-Tek, and she believed that she always would. Her balance, the essence of her that was Chinese, could never be what it was without wreaking vengeance on the person or persons responsible for his murder. That was proving harder than she'd thought. Although the Moon Shadows had a number of enemies within the triads, as well as other eastern and former Soviet bloc countries, she hadn't been able to ferret out the responsible party.

Then, only days ago, the CIA agent Rance Stoddard had set up a meeting with her. According to Stoddard, Syn-Tek

had died while attempting to recover stolen nuclear weapons
from a Russian *mafiya* group. Stoddard had said that Syn-Tek
had agreed to the arrangement to further the Moon Shadow
triad's chances of getting out of Hong Kong intact before encroaching triad families wiped them out. American government assistance was beneficial to relocating Moon Shadow
legitimate business to North America. Work and travel visas
that could later be changed over to citizenship papers came
more easily, as well.

Only three days earlier, Saengkeo had headed up the assault on *Charity's Smile* to recover one of the nuclear
weapons. That effort had been in vain, ruined not only by the
Russian *mafiya* arms brokers aboard the ship, but also by a
single man in black.

The image of the man lifting an arm and grabbing the wing
of the amphibious plane that had rescued him had haunted
Saengkeo's thoughts. She couldn't help wondering if the man
was responsible for Syn-Tek's death. And if he was, she
wanted him dead.

She checked through the security area, handing over her
small handbag and one-piece carryon for scanning.

The big security guard took her cell phone from her handbag. "Could I get you to turn this on for me, ma'am?"

"Of course." Saengkeo pressed the on button and handed
the phone back to the security man.

The guard examined the phone, then flipped the device
over and checked the battery. Satisfied, he handed the phone
back. "Thank you. Have a nice visit."

Saengkeo nodded. Her current papers weren't in her name
and showed her as a Chinese national. The papers that showed
her to be an American citizen would stand up under scrutiny
by most state and federal agencies.

She glanced at the X-ray machine, watching as her handbag and carryon trundled down the conveyor belt and all of

her belongings stood revealed. She stepped through the metal detector frame with only a cursory glance.

At the other end of the conveyor belt, Saengkeo took her cell phone from the plastic basket it had been placed in and switched on the device. When the phone menu came up, she attached it to her belt, then took an earbud from her handbag. She looped the earbud over her left ear and punched the speed-dial function. A man answered the phone on the first ring while she gathered her carryon and handbag.

"Hello," a man answered in English.

"I have arrived," Saengkeo stated.

"We know. A car is waiting for you out front. You will be met."

"What about my guest?"

"We have her."

Saengkeo clicked the phone off. She passed through the terminal and walked toward the waiting area at the front of the building. She took the escalator down, heading for the arrivals concourse.

Johnny Kwan stepped from the side of the escalator before she was halfway down. He nodded slightly, acknowledging her arrival.

Saengkeo's heart knew a flicker of peace and security at the sight of the man, but she walled the feeling away. Until she knew how Syn-Tek had been killed, and who had betrayed him, she didn't dare feel safe.

She nodded back to Kwan.

Johnny Kwan was tall and solid, a handsome man with an easygoing disposition on the surface. Most who knew him never noticed the heavily callused hands or the way his eyes roved constantly while he laughed or smiled or joked. He was the most skilled assassin that Saengkeo had ever met, and he was the greatest and truest friend she and her brother had ever had. Despite the lack of shared blood, Kwan was considered part of the Zhao family. Another turn of the wheel of life, some who knew the family said, and Johnny Kwan would have been one of the family.

He wore jeans, a drab-olive Oxford shirt and a charcoal cargo jacket. Wraparound sunglasses hid his eyes. He carried a simple walking cane that Saengkeo knew he could use as a lethal weapon.

"Your flight was pleasant?" Kwan asked when Saengkeo stepped off the escalator. He made no effort to take her bags, knowing they both preferred him to have his hands free in case there was trouble.

"Yes," she replied. "What about our guest?"

"She is well." Kwan fell into step beside her.

"Have there been any repercussions from the people who held her?"

"No. But she wasn't held the whole time by the Immigration and Naturalization Service."

"We were told that she was." Saengkeo looked straight ahead into the glass doors that opened onto the concourse that ran through the heart of the LAX terminal. Huge concrete elevated streets for the departures level overhead blocked sight of the city and made her feel slightly claustrophobic. Even as heavily populated as Hong Kong was, she had never felt the way the airport had made her feel.

"I know. She says that she wasn't."

"Who had her?"

"She doesn't know."

Saengkeo stepped through the doors. The cool night air swept in from the Pacific Ocean and made her grateful for the jacket.

Cars lined the inner and outer streets where arrivals gathered to find cabs or buses to take them to the car rental agencies in the outlying area around the airport. The stink of exhaust stung Saengkeo's nostrils.

"Where was she kept?" Saengkeo asked.

"She doesn't know."

Irritation filled Saengkeo. Pei-Ling Bao was a friend, a wayward friend perhaps, but there were still pleasant memories from childhood. Only Pei-Ling's refusal to step away from a life of prostitution and drugs had separated them. Occasionally Saengkeo had felt guilt that she had chosen to explore the world rather than stay with her friend. But Pei-Ling hadn't wanted to travel with Saengkeo even though her family had offered to pay her way.

Pei-Ling had worked her way up from the flower boats that serviced tourists in Hong Kong's Aberdeen Harbour. After gaining notoriety, she'd become an adult-film star under various names, working in movies filmed by several triad interests, including—Saengkeo was ashamed to admit—some owned by the Moon Shadows. After that, Pei-Ling had reinvented herself, becoming one of the highest-paid courtesans in Hong Kong.

She reviewed the chaos of the recent past. Nine days ago, Pei-Ling had disappeared without a trace. Ten days ago, Syn-Tek's bullet-riddled body had been found. Five days ago, Wai-Lim Yang had brokered a deal with Saengkeo, revealing that Pei-Ling had been sold to an American-located triad specializing in prostitution. Later that same day, CIA agent Rance Stoddard had revealed that Syn-Tek had been killed during a raid that had netted the American government one of the three missing nuclear devices that had been sold to Middle Eastern terrorists. Three days ago, Saengkeo had been assigned to recover one of the last two devices, only to be thwarted by the man in black in the Indian Ocean.

She saw the man again in her mind's eye. He had looked savage and primeval draped with weapons and plucked from the sea by the floatplane.

Kwan touched Saengkeo's elbow, stopping her at the curb.

A long navy blue Mercedes limousine slid to a smooth stop. The driver hopped out immediately and opened the rear passenger door. He was one of Kwan's handpicked men and had arrived with Kwan earlier that day. Saengkeo had chosen to fly later in order to settle business arrangements amid the triad families. Even in the middle of chaos, business had to go on.

Kwan had wanted the extra time to check out the lay of the land. The INS wasn't in the habit of holding on to a person judged to be an undesirable alien. Only Saengkeo's L.A.-based attorneys had arranged dispensation in the case, citing a need to have Pei-Ling treated by a physician before deporting her. After all, as the attorneys had pointed out, Pei-Ling Bao had been kidnapped at gunpoint and transported to first Mexico then into the United States without either her consent or her knowledge.

There had been several other women in the group transported by the Soaring Dragons, a young hard-core Chinese organized-crime group that claimed affiliation with the Big Circle Society. That claim, according to the research Johnny Kwan had done, wasn't completely supported. The Big Circle Society hadn't claimed the affiliation existed upon discreet inquiry through a third-party source.

Then again, the Big Circle Society would be careful in such a situation. The sexual-slavery aspects of the arrests by Border Patrol agents in Arizona had captured a huge amount of media attention.

Saengkeo slid over to the seat behind the driver. Kwan got in beside her.

Before she reached for the seat belt, Saengkeo popped out the hidden cache beneath the seat. She reached into the small recess and took out the double shoulder holster rig that held twin .40-caliber Walther Model P-990 QPQs. They were her weapons of choice, and she kept them stashed wherever her family business took her. She slipped off her jacket, trusting the smoke-tinted windows to keep any curious passersby from seeing her, then shrugged into the shoulder holster. Her current ID also carried a gun permit in L.A. as part of the package. She racked the slides, putting a live shell under the firing pins, then eased the hammers back down.

Kwan pulled on a double shoulder holster rig containing Kimber Ultra Ten II semiautomatic pistols with low-profile sights. Both weapons were chambered in .45 ACP and featured 14-round magazines. Saengkeo knew that because Kwan had tried to get her to change her own choice of weapons.

"Someone had Pei-Ling for the past few days," Saengkeo said.

"Yes," Kwan agreed. "But I have been unable to find out who. The American government isn't very forthcoming with their information. In addition, I believe Pei-Ling has been *lost* in their records for some time."

"With the Americans, that is possible."

"Possible," Kwan said, "but I don't believe it."

The driver stepped back to his side of the car and got in. A moment later, the limousine glided powerfully from the curb, merging with the heavy traffic.

"Where does Pei-Ling think she was?" Saengkeo asked.

Kwan grimaced as he gazed outside his window. Even when they were all younger, he had never cared for Pei-Ling. "She believes she was held by the INS."

"The attorneys said she was drugged."

"Drugs are a way of life for her," Kwan said unkindly. "The Soaring Dragons rendered her unconscious. When she recovered, she was forced to go without medical help for her withdrawal pains. She wasn't given anything until your lawyers interceded on her behalf. She's still not happy."

"How did the Border Patrol find out the Soaring Dragons had her?"

"The Border Patrol was working off routine information," Kwan said. "But they didn't actually save her. The Soaring Dragons managed to kill several of the Border Patrol."

Saengkeo looked at Kwan, who gazed back at her. The black lenses of his sunglasses hid any emotion, though Saengkeo felt certain none would have been revealed anyway.

"Who saved Pei-Ling?" Saengkeo asked.

"A man dressed all in black."

"Did she identify this man?"

"No."

"Did Pei-Ling see this man among the INS personnel later?"

"No. But he questioned her at length in a hotel room in Scottsdale, Arizona. By himself."

Saengkeo digested that. "A proper INS agent or a Border Patrol guard wouldn't have risked such exposure to charges."

"No," Kwan agreed.

However, Saengkeo was aware that they both knew INS agents and Border Patrol guards had done much worse at times. No matter what agency, no matter what country, there were always infractions and abuses. Those were the cracks professional criminals and crime organizations utilized to carry on business.

"He wasn't a proper INS agent or a Border Patrol guard," Saengkeo said, looking back at the traffic. The limousine halted momentarily at the on-ramp to southbound Sepulveda Boulevard, then joined the slow-moving traffic.

"No."

"Do you think he is the same man?"

Kwan appeared to consider the question. He knew which man she meant. "No," Kwan said. "Perhaps there was time for that man to have left Scottsdale, Arizona, and made the jump into the Indian Ocean to intercept the ship, but if that is the case, he must be well-informed."

"Better than we are informed." They rode in silence. Her mind worked at the events, matching them up, wondering if the same man in black had been in both places. Fatigue ate into her. She had slept a little in the first-class accommodations aboard the jet from Hong Kong, but not much. Bruises lingered over her body where bullets had impacted against her Kevlar armor while on *Charity's Smile*.

During her early years, Saengkeo hadn't known all the things that Johnny Kwan had been trained for. She had been fifteen when she'd first discovered what he was capable of. Kwan had been twenty. Two men had tried to kidnap her, and Kwan had killed them both—without hesitation and without mercy. Saengkeo had never seen a person die violently until that time. For a number of years, she'd had nightmares about the experience, and she'd thought of Johnny Kwan as an angel of death.

Until the night on board *Charity's Smile*, Saengkeo had never seen anyone who could rival the impression Kwan had given her. In the years since that time, she'd killed a number of times herself. Sometimes she'd killed with Kwan at her side, trusting him to be there.

At the end of Sepulveda Boulevard, the limousine driver turned east onto 105. Kwan had checked Pei-Ling into a hotel under another name along the Los Angeles Harbor.

The phone that connected the back of the car with the driver buzzed for attention.

Kwan lifted the receiver, listened briefly, then put the instrument away. He spoke without looking at Saengkeo. "It appears that we are being followed."

Kong Kong

RANCE STODDARD PACED the floor in front of the rows of monitors that connected him to different venues of the operations he was responsible for while dealing with the situation in Hong Kong regarding the Chinese government and the triad crime cartels. When he'd first been made agent-in-charge in the Asian theater, he hadn't known keeping all the balls in the air was going to require as much energy or so much of his attention.

Of course, he hadn't counted on losing Syn-Tek Zhao and dealing with his sister. Or the problem that Jacy Corbin possibly presented. And he damn well hadn't counted on the involvement of the team that had rescued Pei-Ling Bao and interfered with the recovery of the nuclear weapon aboard *Charity's Smile*.

"Do you know this woman?" David Kelso nodded toward the screen that had captured Stoddard's attention.

"Karin Bristow," Stoddard said. "She's old-line CIA. She worked in East Germany before the Wall fell and everything went to hell there."

Kelso scratched his stubbled chin. His attention remained rapt on the monitor screen. "Is she going to kill this guy?"

On the screen, Karin Bristow questioned the man she'd captured in the Nautilus Club in Vancouver, British Columbia. One of the two agents with her used a small wireless digital video camera to transmit the scene from the building's maintenance room. The streaming video maintained remarkable clarity with something more than a half-second delay.

"Do you think she's going to kill that man?" Stoddard asked.

Kelso hesitated. "Maybe."

The man's right cheek had swollen almost enough to close his eye. Bruises mottled the entire side of the man's face. Blood trickled down his chin from his split lip.

"Let's hope he thinks so, too," Stoddard said.

"You didn't answer my question," Kelso stated.

"Queasy?"

"I've never shot anyone that wasn't shooting back at me or someone I was partnered with," Kelso admitted. "Cold-blooded wet work isn't my cup of tea."

"Thankfully, Karin has no such qualms."

"Neither does Jacy," Kelso said.

"No," Stoddard agreed. "Neither does Corbin." He blew out his breath, trying in vain to release some of the pent-up tension filling his body. The way he was going, he wasn't going to live long enough to spend the retirement fund he was putting together. "To answer your question, no, Karin's not going to kill that man. Unless she's ordered to."

"And if she's ordered to?"

"Then he goes out like a light switch."

Kelso shook his head. "So how well do you know this woman?"

"Back in the day, I knew her well. I still know her well enough to ask her to take care of this end of things for us and have her accept."

"Have you ever noticed you have a thing for homicidal women?"

"Part of the thrill. You never know if you're going to wake up when you sleep with them." Stoddard studied the drama playing out on the screen. He wished the audio capability had come on-line, but pumping the video feed through was risky enough without layering in an audio track.

An icon suddenly flashed on the computer monitor directly in front of Kelso. "The Vancouver team just breached the building's security camera systems."

Stoddard looked the question at the other man.

Kelso tapped keys, shifting the duplicated images of the maintenance room scene to other views. "We've got access to the other cameras throughout the building. We can look for the fly-guy's partner."

"Try Eric Barnes's office," Stoddard suggested.

Kelso tapped the keyboard again, watching the screens for results. The monitor in front of him held a camera key.

The camera key was no mystery, Stoddard knew. Money greased wheels in the security business, and a few of the people in that business worked both ends against the people they protected to earn the most they could. Sometimes security people were the best blackmailers. One of the security corporation's officers was a known snitch for the Vancouver Police Department, as well as for international traffickers in secrets.

When one of the monitors cleared with an image of a man dressed in black in the shadows of an office room, Stoddard leaned forward with interest. The camera was set up high on the wall and provided a fish-eye view of the room. The black-clad man raised the big pistol he carried and fired quickly. Yellow muzzle-flashes spit from the barrel.

"That looks like the pictures of the guy at the Russian cargo ship," Kelso commented.

"Can't be," Stoddard said. "There has to be more than two guys involved in this operation."

Kelso nodded to the monitor showing the interrogation taking place in the building's maintenance room. "You're looking at one of the guys there. Why couldn't the other one be there?"

"The operation has to be bigger than two men." Stoddard watched as the black-clad man grabbed the arm of a woman and hustled her toward the window. "Who is the woman?"

"I don't know." Kelso tapped a key. A moment later, a still image of the scene in the building office formed on a monitor. He worked the trackball, cutting and cropping the image of the woman. He tapped more keys. "But we'll find out."

In the next instant, the black-clad man passed the woman out the window and followed after her. Stoddard watched with growing interest.

"Shouldn't have gone outside the building," Kelso commented. "He's going to be a sitting duck when Barnes's support team get there."

Stoddard said nothing. He remembered the lightning attack that had taken place aboard *Charity's Smile*. The man on the monitor wasn't the type to get himself into a situation without a backup plan.

In the next instant, an explosion lit up the computer monitor. Stoddard had the fleeting impression of a flaming body being thrown out the window, then the screen went black. He glanced at the other monitors cycling through the building's security zones, making certain the whole system hadn't shut down.

"What happened?" Stoddard asked.

"An explosion," Kelso answered.

Stoddard watched the cycling images. "Are there any cameras outside the building?"

"None that we can access."

Stoddard studied the images. "Barnes is dead."

"And how," Kelso agreed, bringing up a monitor view of the black-clad man stepping across Barnes's corpse.

This time Stoddard saw the man shove the shaped charge onto the door frame. The view also showed the gaping wound in the side of Barnes's head. Even if the man hadn't been dead, the explosion that had rocked the room no doubt would have killed him.

"The police?" Stoddard asked.

"Already on their way, I'm told. Be there in a few minutes."

Stoddard looked back at the interrogation Karin Bristow was conducting. "That man will come here. To rescue his friend. He has no choice." He nodded at the keyboard. "Alert the Vancouver teams. Tell them that he's on his way."

"They've seen the same footage that we have."

"Tell them," Stoddard ordered.

Then the monitors relaying the video feeds from the building in Vancouver, British Columbia, flickered and filled with gray-and-white snow.

Kelso cursed and quickly worked the keyboard. Lines of text filled the computer screen in front of him. "Somebody shut us down."

"Who?"

"I don't know," Kelso said. "They tripped a firewall-intrusive countermeasure. They were trying to get inside our system."

"Did they?"

"I don't think so." Kelso tapped the keys. New lines of script appeared on the monitor. "I'm shutting down the phone connections we had open to British Columbia." He glanced up, checking the blank monitors. "Looks like they've already jettisoned us from most of them."

"Can you tell where the attack originated from?"

Kelso shrugged. "Maybe in a little while. But an attack like this?" He shook his head. "Guys that can do this are phantom crackers. They come and go without leaving a trace."

Stoddard considered that, feeling a sinking sensation in the pit of his stomach. Someone was closing in on his operation, and that someone was good. "Find out what you can."

Kelso nodded and bent to the task.

Irritated and anxious, Stoddard watched the remaining screens. Some of them peered into homes and businesses owned by Chinese triad members he had under surveillance. Saengkeo Zhao's meeting with the triads four days ago had spawned new problems. Syn-Tek Zhao's death had inspired some of the triad families, like Wai-Lim Yang's Black Swans, to try to take over some of the Moon Shadow territory. And Saengkeo's aggressive behavior during the recent summit meeting had incited harsh feelings toward her.

As a result, knowing Saengkeo had stolen away from Hong Kong to attempt the retrieval of Pei-Ling Bao in the United States, Stoddard had put teams on her around the clock. As

soon as she had landed at LAX, teams had fallen into position to watch her. Stoddard had also asked for and gotten
satellite access to keep a visual tag on the woman.

On the screen dedicated to Saengkeo, Stoddard watched
the enhanced image of the sleek limousine that had picked the
woman up at LAX and was now driving east on 105 toward
110 South. In disbelief, he saw the limousine suddenly speed
up. A moment later a vehicle rocketed forward, gaining
ground quickly and overtaking the limousine. Just as abruptly,
the vehicle drew even with the limousine and bright muzzle-
flashes jumped from the passenger-side window.

In response the limousine slid off the highway and plunged
cross-country.

9

Vancouver, British Columbia

Bolan stepped outside the sixth-floor office, Desert Eagle up and probing. De-Ying Wu stayed close behind him, but he kept an eye on her, too. She'd taken the blistering attack on the floor below in stride, proving herself impressively resilient.

"Striker," Barbara Price spoke over the headset. "We discovered an outside source peeking into events taking place there through a computer link. We tracked the signal back to Hong Kong before we lost it."

"Our primary target in Hong Kong?" Bolan walked quickly, avoiding the mall-like area between the shops that were still open on the sixth floor.

"We can't say for sure. We're still working with what little we did get. The surprising thing is that the computer link was shifting through satellite arrays used by our government."

"Affirmative," Bolan responded. His mind spun through the directions Price had given him to the maintenance room where Grimaldi was being held captive.

Wu followed him, and Bolan was surprised to see that the woman showed such dogged determination to stay with him. He'd fully expected her to run for cover at the first opportunity. Of course, the fact that Barnes's security people might have stopped her was incentive enough to keep her with the Executioner.

Less than a minute later, Bolan was in the hallway where the maintenance room was. He read the red-and-white plaque across the door: Maintenance Authorized Personnel Only.

"Stony Base," Bolan said, "confirm Mustang's presence and Striker's position outside the room."

"Presence confirmed," Price said. "Position confirmed. He's still alive for the moment, but things aren't looking good in there."

"You still have no contact with his headset?"

"No."

"Three people are inside with Mustang," Bolan stated.

"Correct, Striker. Three. And those three are heavily armed. The woman is in front of Mustang. One man is behind her, nearest the door. The door opens to the right. The other man is standing to the left as you open the door."

"Understood."

"They're also probably off-limits."

Bolan had that figured. "Off-limits" meant that the three people were either Canadian law enforcement or American law enforcement. Either way, he couldn't fire on them.

He stepped close to the maintenance door. Echoes from the people gathered at shops farther down rolled over him. All the shoppers were aware of the explosion that had taken place. The soldier felt bad about the fear that his actions had inspired, but there had been no way around it.

He tried the door but found it locked. The voices coming from inside sounded muted, distant. Thankfully, the door wasn't meant as anything more than a strong deterrent. He glanced at the woman, waving her back against the wall ten feet down from the door.

Stepping back from the door, Bolan locked on the Desert Eagle's safety. He lifted his foot and drove it into the door, splintering the hinges and driving the door inside as the lock gave way. He followed the door inside, trusting the Kevlar armor in case any shots were fired. If he didn't move quickly enough, he knew that Grimaldi was at risk anyway.

The man standing in front of the woman confronting Grimaldi with a small pistol turned, accidentally stepping into the woman's line of fire.

The Executioner grabbed the man's jacket in his free hand and drove him backward into the woman. She fired anyway, and the round caught the man in the shoulder in a spray of torn material and blood that flecked Bolan's face. Everything happened so fast that the man didn't even have time to cry out.

The man's weight barreled over the woman, knocking her back and to one side as he stumbled and went down, grabbing his wounded shoulder. The woman pushed at the man with her free hand, trying to disentangle herself from him and get her pistol in the clear. Bolan reached for her, caught the pistol and plucked it from her grip. The barrel spit flame, but the round impacted harmlessly against the wall behind the Executioner.

He took in Grimaldi's battered face in a second and knew that the pilot had been worked over with a gun butt. Still moving, Bolan caught the woman across the face with a forearm shiver that lifted her from her feet. He turned toward the remaining man.

The guy was slow, going for a pistol holstered high over his right hip. Bolan reached him before the weapon cleared leather. A backhand blow against the temple with the Desert Eagle corkscrewed the man around and sent him to an unconscious heap on the floor. At the worst, he had a concussion, but he was still alive.

"Sarge!" Grimaldi called out in warning before Bolan could turn.

Spinning, the Executioner found the woman in full charge, a short, triangular fighting knife clasped between the third and fourth fingers of her right hand. The blade was designed to open up wounds that didn't close so the injured party would bleed out in seconds.

Before the woman reached Bolan, De-Ying Wu stepped into the room, grabbed a mop and thrust the handle between the attacking woman's legs. The woman tripped and rolled acrobatically, changing course for Wu. Bolan guessed that the woman intended to take Wu as a hostage.

Wu set herself in a martial-arts stance, open hands lifted before her, then stepped in with a front kick to her adversary's face. The woman's headlong rush carried her to Wu as the smaller woman twisted away, but it was only pent-up motion. She sprawled to the floor and didn't get back up.

Sliding a Tanto blade from his boot, Bolan sliced through the plastic cuffs holding Grimaldi prisoner. "Are you okay?" the Executioner asked.

"I've been better," Grimaldi admitted.

Bolan nodded at the three unconscious people. "Who are your playmates?"

"Beats me." Grimaldi touched his face. "Literally."

Kneeling, Bolan shoved the Desert Eagle's barrel against the wounded man's forehead.

The man groaned in pain but lay back with his hands pushed away from his body.

Bolan quickly went through the man's clothing, taking his wallet and emptying his pockets. The soldier placed everything in a drawstring pouch he took from a thigh pocket of his pants.

"Who are you?" Bolan asked the man.

"One of the last guys you should have ever fucked with," the man snarled in a false show of bravado.

"We'll find out," Bolan said.

"They knew who you are," the man threatened. "Someone will come after you. One of these days, when you least expect it, someone will be over your shoulder and you'll never see it coming."

Bolan nodded. Time was passing, and he knew he was pushing the envelope on the mission. Eliminating Eric Barnes, making his presence known in Vancouver—that was all he'd set out to do. There were a lot of other places to be before morning.

Grimaldi searched the unconscious man. Wu, surprisingly, went through the unconscious woman's clothing, pocketing everything she found.

Standing, Bolan stepped over to the notebook computer-cell phone combo on the worktable. He shut down the devices, placing the phone in a pocket and tucking the computer under his arm. He leathered the Desert Eagle, then took out a small digital camera and snapped pictures of the three people who had captured Grimaldi.

"Time to go, Striker," Price called over the headset. "Two marked police cars are out in front of the building. Backup units are less than a minute away."

"On our way," Bolan said.

He looked at Wu. "I want to talk to you, but the choice is yours."

"You can get out of this building without getting caught by the police?" Wu asked.

"Yeah."

The woman hesitated only a moment. "I'd rather not get questioned all night, and I'm probably about as keen on getting caught here as you are."

"Then stay close," Bolan advised her. "We're going to be

moving quick." He turned and left the maintenance room, getting instructions from Price regarding one of the escape routes they'd laid out from the building.

Los Angeles, California

"DOWN!" Johnny Kwan yelled.

Saengkeo Zhao was already in motion. She'd seen the man wielding the Ingram MAC-10 in the passenger seat of the small sedan as he'd poked the wicked snout of the machine pistol through the window toward the limousine.

Forty-five-caliber hail shattered the limousine's windows. Some of the rounds tore through the windows on the other side of the luxury car, but a few of them bounced in the vehicle's interior. One of the rounds gouged through the back of her left thigh while another burned across the back of her neck. Both Walther Model P-990s were in her hands as she flung herself against the seat. Thunder rolled through the limousine's interior.

Kwan pulled a cell phone from inside his jacket and pressed a button. Before the call had time to complete, the car beside the limousine veered over into the luxury vehicle. Perhaps the limo's bulk and pent-up speed would have held it on course against the weight and push of the other vehicle, but the gunner in the passenger seat targeted the limo driver.

The driver's head exploded in a rush of scarlet that painted the inside of the windshield. Abruptly the vehicle left the highway, careening across the shoulder.

Highway 105 was heavily traveled during the entire day. A number of motorists were still making their way home or to their jobs. Horns blared as they sped by. Other vehicles threaded through the traffic, targeting the limousine.

The luxury car rolled to a stop amid a roiling dust cloud.

"Get out," Kwan stated calmly, gesturing to the door on Saengkeo's side.

Saengkeo reached up and smashed the interior dome light with the butt of the Walther in her right hand. Even as the pieces of protective plastic and the tiny glass shards showered down, she caught the door latch with her little finger and pushed it open. She broke into a run, taking in the uneven terrain that made up the highway shoulder.

The whine of motorcycle engines cut through the road noises. Up on 105, traffic came to a standstill as motorists braked to gawk at the action taking place.

The car that had rammed the limousine had continued along the highway. White reverse lights flared briefly, then the vehicle pulled off-road and swung around toward the limousine.

Kwan joined Saengkeo. "This way."

The woman turned and followed him, sprinting into the brush at the side of the road. Downtown Los Angeles was a bright glow against the dark night farther north. Her breath ripped through her lungs in explosive gasps, but her blood moved readily. Sitting in the jet for the past several hours hadn't prepared her to be physical at a moment's notice.

"Who are they?" Saengkeo demanded.

"I don't know," Kwan answered. "I had two blocker vehicles running in tandem to us. Both of them were taken out at the same time that we were forced off the road. There are other cars on the way."

Saengkeo swept her eyes across the night-shadowed countryside. If the man in black had stepped from the darkness at that moment, she wouldn't have been surprised. There was a tie between them; she knew that with a certainty.

The car that had rammed them from the road roared across the broken terrain.

Kwan led the way to a copse of trees growing so closely together that the car wouldn't be able to squeeze through. He lifted his pistols and fired on the run. Not all of the bullets struck the car as it approached, but several of the rounds struck sparks or pockmarked the windshield.

The passenger shoved his way through the window and sat in a half crouch, looped over the top. He brought the Ingram to bear, muzzle-flashes winking rapidly. A line of bullets tore through the ground, then tracked up the trees and through the branches above Saengkeo's head.

Reaching the first tree, Saengkeo stepped behind the trunk and swung around with the Walthers extended. She fired from the point, aiming by experience and instinct at the gunner's exposed head and shoulders.

Some of the bullets struck the driver's side, but at least one snapped into the gunner's head. The car continued tearing across the slight hillside, but the gunner dropped to the ground and didn't move.

Kwan placed his back to another tree. A phone earbud hung from one ear, the connecting cord running down to the phone in his pocket. He talked quickly and quietly, evidently directing the men he had assigned to covering them. He dropped the magazine from one of the Kimber semiautomatic pistols and thumbed fresh cartridges from an ammo bag at his waist while he held the other pistol tucked into his armpit.

Saengkeo replaced both of her weapons' magazines, then combined the partially spent magazines into a completely filled one with a couple loose rounds.

"They're on their way," Kwan said.

Saengkeo nodded, keeping her attention on the bashed car coming around in a circle before the trees. Other gunners moved in the back of the vehicle. The car swept by again, and the gunner unleashed a spray of bullets.

Leaves and small branches dropped down like party confetti. Long splinters ripped from the tree Saengkeo used for cover. Other trees took similar hits, and white patches stood out against the dark bark.

Saengkeo waited until the car passed, then looked at Kwan. "Cover me."

"What—"

Not giving Kwan the chance to finish his question, Saengkeo sprinted toward the fallen gunner. She stayed low and hoped she was moving too fast for the driver or the other gunners to notice. Behind her, the engine revved and tires screamed against the ground.

Kwan stepped from cover and shoved both pistols in front of him. Muzzle-flashes blazed from the barrels, and the .45 ACP rounds hammered the body of the car. Following his instinct for self-preservation, the car's driver yanked hard to the left, pulling the vehicle out of line of attack against Saengkeo.

She ran, stretching her legs, churning across the uneven ground. She reached the man she'd killed, shoved her left-hand Walther into shoulder leather and grabbed a fistful of the man's lightweight jacket. Dropping to her knees, she set herself and yanked.

The body rolled over. Moonlight and indirect light from the highway revealed the dead man's features. He looked as if he might have been twenty. Temporary dye turned his hair green. Black eyeliner outlined his wide and staring eyes, and his lips were painted a brilliant red. He wore a black silk shirt over a white T-shirt.

Saengkeo's bullet had torn his throat out, killing him nearly instantly. The blood glistened over his shoulders and had stained the front of his shirts.

She distanced herself from the young man's age. In the United States and China, the young fighters serving the various triads were the first to fall. Those numbers increased dramatically among the Asian youth gangs that tried to make it on their own, or tried to prove their worth to the more powerful entities like the Big Circle Society or the United Bamboo families.

The chops, tattoos announcing his triad affiliation, on the side of his neck claimed him as a member of the Steel Tigers. The Steel Tigers were an L.A.-based youth group that specialized in car-jackings and home burglaries. They were hardcore, hanging on to mythical loyalties that some said involved drinking blood from the masters they swore loyalty to. Leaving the Steel Tigers was a death sentence. The only future was eventual death.

The Ingram MAC-10 lay on the ground beside the corpse.

Saengkeo searched the body, turning up five spare magazines for the machine pistol. She shoved four of them into her jacket pocket, then changed out the 30-round magazine. Holstering her other Walther, she hefted the machine pistol in both hands and spun to face the car.

"Look out!" Kwan yelled, pistols cracking in both his fists.

Pushing herself to her feet, Saengkeo raised the MAC-10 and squeezed the trigger. The machine pistol bucked in her hands, squirming like a live thing trying to burst free.

The initial bullets chopped grass in front of the approaching car, but the recoil pushed the Ingram higher until the rounds hammered through the windshield. Saengkeo targeted the driver, forcing herself not to think of how young he probably was.

She threw herself aside at the last minute just after the Ingram cycled dry. A wall of grass and dust whipped across her, taking her breath for just an instant. She rolled, arched her body and came to her feet as three motorcycles roared over the highway embankment.

The motorcycles' lights strobed the night as they hung in flight for a moment, then they stuttered as the two-wheeled vehicles crashed to the earth again. Two riders sat on each motorcycle. The ones in the back had machine pistols, aimed at Saengkeo.

Knowing she would never reach the safety of the trees, Saengkeo dropped the empty magazine from the MAC-10 and shoved another stick into the machine pistol's grip. She readied the weapon, then sprinted right at the lead motorcycle. From the corner of her eye, she saw that the sedan that had attacked the limousine had crashed against the trees to her right.

The distance between Saengkeo and the lead motorcycle evaporated. She felt the wind from bullets cut the air beside her head. Another round caught the tail of her jacket, tearing through with a jerk. At the last moment, she threw herself into the air, praying that she'd gotten the timing right.

She flipped, watching the lead motorcycle shoot across the ground under her. Angling her body, she twisted in the air and landed on her feet. She raised the MAC-10 and fired, sweeping a figure eight from left to right and back again.

Two of the motorcycles tumbled end over end as the drivers lost control or were killed. Kwan targeted the remaining motorcycle and blasted both riders from the seat.

In the next instant, another wave of motorcycle riders shot over the embankment. They landed on the hillside, rear tires spinning and tearing turf away in clumps.

Saengkeo sprinted for the stalled sedan as bullets thudded into the ground where she'd been standing. She thumbed the Ingram's magazine release and shoved in a fresh clip. Six feet from the sedan, she launched herself into the air again, whipping her feet out in front of her and skidding across the sedan's engine hood.

A hail of bullets drummed across the car, tearing through the sheet metal and punching out the remaining glass in the windows. Saengkeo dropped to the ground on the other side of the car. Bullets whined through the air above her head, then fistfuls of square-cut safety glass blew over her.

She pushed her back against the car, making herself into as small a target as she could, taking advantage of every inch of cover the vehicle offered. The sedan wobbled, and the sound of bullet impacts filled Saengkeo's ears.

A motorcycle engine whined, and a shadow knifed through the air above Saengkeo, a figure at the back firing a sustained burst from a machine pistol. The muzzle-flashes lit up the two leather-clad gang members on the motorcycle.

Saengkeo raised the Ingram and unleashed a burst by sheer instinct, leading the motorcycle a little. Bullets struck sparks from the angled exhaust pipe on the bike's right, then a few others ripped into the gas tank.

The sparks ignited the gasoline immediately, and the motorcycle became a hurtling fireball that smashed against the ground. Both riders rolled free, flames washing over their bodies.

Saengkeo fired into both riders, hammering them into stillness. At her side, the car door opened and another Steel Tigers gang member staggered out with his arm thrust through the broken glass of the door window. He fired twice, missing Saengkeo with both shots.

Kicking upward, she caught her adversary's wrist and sent his weapon flying. Undaunted, he shoved his way around the door and came at her. He swept a stiletto from one of his jacket sleeves, the naked blade gleaming in the moonlight as it swept toward his victim.

Flipping backward, Saengkeo rolled lithely to her feet, then launched a back roundhouse kick that slammed against the man's wrist. He stubbornly held on to the knife and threw himself at her.

Saengkeo blocked the knife attack with the blunt, angular shape of the MAC-10. Metal grated as the knife slid along the machine pistol. From the corner of her eye, she saw another motorcycle circle the back of the sedan. The motorcycle's rear tire skidded sideways as the driver braked to a halt. The passenger unlimbered an Uzi and opened fire.

Still blocking the knife thrust, Saengkeo stepped into her opponent's embrace. A cruel smile crossed the man's face for just an instant, then a fusillade of bullets slammed into his back from his fellow Steel Tigers. Life was cheap on the streets, and success was measured in blood and kills.

Saengkeo stayed behind the dying man and lifted the MAC-10 under one of his arms. She squeezed the trigger and tracked a stream of bullets up the motorcycle and swept the driver and rider. The bodies fell and the machine tumbled over, sputtered and died.

Pushing the corpse from her, Saengkeo dumped the MAC-10's clip and fed in a fresh one. Her heartbeat roared in her ears. She was conscious of being covered in her blood, as well as the blood of others. Glancing around, she spotted Kwan charging across the ground toward her.

The motorcycles circled for another pass. Their headlights flashed across Saengkeo's eyes, robbing her of her night vision.

"Help is on the way," Kwan said. He knelt beside the car for a moment. A knife flashed in his hand, and the smell of pungent gasoline filled Saengkeo's nostrils. He pushed her into motion. "Go. Toward the highway. The blocker cars have been delayed by the traffic and by our attackers. Maybe we can use the traffic against them."

Saengkeo nodded and started up the hill. The motorcycle engines revved behind her, and she knew they were closing in again. Glancing over her shoulder, she saw Kwan flick a lighter to life then throw it into the puddle of liquid gathering under the car.

A mist of yellow-and-blue flames twisted across the puddled gasoline's surface, then climbed up under the car. Kwan took four steps before the explosion occurred.

What felt like a sledgehammer slammed between Saengkeo's shoulder blades and knocked her from her feet. She went down in dry grass that scratched her face.

The car exploded, leaping from the ground. Flames spread ten feet in either direction, quickly claiming the dry grass that covered the hillside, and fiery debris filled the sky.

Kwan caught Saengkeo by the elbow. "Let's go. That will only buy us a little time."

Saengkeo knew Kwan's assessment was true. The flames robbed the night vision of the Steel Tigers, too, and—to a degree—masked their escape up the hillside. She ran, breathing hard now, her senses reeling. Smoke clogged her throat and burned her lungs.

At the top of the hillside, traffic had come to a standstill in places, but a line surged around the stalled cars just the same. The fire would draw the police, and although Saengkeo welcomed the eventual LAPD presence as another source of aid, she knew police investigators would have a number of questions, as well.

Kwan talked rapidly over the cell phone. The earbud cord swung at the side of his face, smearing the blood that dripped from his scalp. He gave directions to the blocker cars as he searched for them in the confusion of traffic.

Before Saengkeo could get her bearings, a small cluster of motorcycle riders roared through the stopped cars. Their headlights swept over Saengkeo and Kwan, and muzzle-flashes lit up the night again.

Kwan started to run toward the cars.

"No!" Saengkeo ordered. She stared into the cherubic face of a small child pressed against the window of a van in front of her. "We'll go back down the hill."

"We won't be able to escape them there," Kwan objected.

"I'm not going to endanger any of these people." Saengkeo ran down the hillside, aiming for the copse of trees.

The motorcycles followed at once, rapidly closing the distance.

Saengkeo knew she would never reach the trees. She stopped and turned, raising the MAC-10. Johnny Kwan took up a position at her side, standing slightly before her to better protect her.

The five motorcycles left the highway and roared down the hillside. Before they did more than touch the ground again, an engine roared behind them, masking even the high-pitched two-cycle noise of the motorcycle engines. Then a black Suburban SUV launched from the highway hillside like a rocket. Disbelief filled Saengkeo as she watched the vehicle sail through the air and land in the middle of the motorcycles like a lion attacking a herd of unsuspecting antelope.

The motorcycles went down under the assault like scythed wheat.

For a moment Saengkeo thought the Suburban was going to flip over. The vehicle rose high on the right two wheels, then came down hard. The four-wheel-drive chewed into the earth as the driver aimed the vehicle at Saengkeo.

Taking advantage of the brief respite, Saengkeo and Kwan reached the treeline. She raised the machine pistol and watched the big Suburban bearing down on them. Behind the monstrous vehicle, a handful of motorcycles vectored in on their position.

The Suburban skidded to a halt sideways with the passenger-side door facing Saengkeo. The door opened, revealing the young, hard-bodied blond woman at the wheel. She wore a sapphire-blue turtleneck and khaki pants. A cigarette was clamped tightly between her lips, and the coal glowed bright orange for a moment. A shoulder holster rig showed starkly against the sapphire turtleneck.

The woman plucked the cigarette from her mouth and flicked it through the door. The cigarette hit the door frame and scattered miniature orange embers across the breeze.

"So," the woman said, "you gonna get in the car? Or are you gonna fuck up my big rescue?"

10

"Who are you?" Kwan demanded. He aimed both Kimber Ultra Ten II pistols at the woman.

"My name is Jacy Corbin," she answered, looking at Saengkeo. "I work with CIA Special Agent-in-Charge Rance Stoddard, and if you guys are wired or have bugs on you, I just fucked up big time."

Shots from the approaching motorcycles rang out but struck the Suburban without causing any damage. The vehicle was evidently heavily armored.

"How did you—?" Kwan started.

"Fuck me!" Jacy exploded, losing a little of her relaxed demeanor. "We're not exactly starring in an episode of *Biography* here. Get in the vehicle or die."

Kwan didn't appear willing.

"Get in the car," Saengkeo said in English, not wanting to take the chance that the CIA agent didn't speak Chinese. She stepped into the passenger seat of the high vehicle while Kwan climbed into the rear section.

"Hang on," Corbin advised. She pulled the transmission lever into Low and stomped the accelerator. Cutting the wheel around hard, she headed back toward the speeding Steel Tigers motorcyclists. Bullets flattened against the windshield, creating minute cracks but not penetrating. "One of our special modifieds. This bitch is a rolling dreadnought."

The motorcycles split before her. One of them pulled away too late. The Suburban's front bumper clipped the motorcycle's rear tire and knocked the bike spinning to the ground.

Shots continued to hammer the Suburban, striking like leaden rain.

Without hesitation, Jacy Corbin sped up the hillside. She cut the wheel sharply and pulled into the eastbound traffic, staying on the shoulder and roaring past the stalled traffic.

"So where to?" Jacy asked.

Saengkeo was aware of Kwan talking quickly in the back seat, relaying orders over the cell phone. She didn't respond.

"L.A. Harbor, right?" Jacy asked. "Where you've got the Pei-Ling woman stashed."

"How did you know that?" Saengkeo asked.

Corbin sighed, took out a cigarette pack and lit one up. "Look around, Miss Zhao. I'm not the only one that knows your business. In case you didn't notice it, you were set up tonight. You were supposed to have died in that firefight back there."

"I don't have enemies among the Steel Tigers."

"The Steel Tigers are a mercenary group," Corbin said. "They get an erection any time one of the larger triads mention the possibility of annexing them and protecting them from the other bottom feeders out here." The woman glanced at Saengkeo. "You've got enemies. One of them hired the

Steel Tigers to bury you. Maybe you should concentrate on who did that."

"Maybe," Saengkeo said, "I should concentrate on why they would wait until I was over here."

"Because of Pei-Ling," Corbin said. She nodded. "Have you talked to her yet?"

"You don't know?"

Corbin pulled into the highway traffic, cutting across a lane and drawing an irritated honk. "I don't know everything, Miss Zhao. I only figured maybe you could use someone to watch your back while you were here."

"Or maybe you figured you could spy on me."

A small, sad smile framed Corbin's mouth. "Touché. Funny how being around Stoddard makes you paranoid, isn't it?"

"What does he know about my brother's death?"

Corbin regarded her. "What has he told you?"

"That Syn-Tek was killed while working for him."

"He was."

"By whom?"

"I don't know." Corbin glanced in the rearview mirror. "We've got a tail. Hang on."

Turning in her seat, Saengkeo searched the traffic behind them. She spotted the two motorcycles trailing them almost effortlessly through the congested traffic.

Corbin pulled back onto the highway's shoulder, tossed her cigarette out the window, then reached under the dashboard and pressed a button.

Abruptly Saengkeo was shoved back into her seat with stunning force. The Suburban's engine kicked up the noise index to near jet-engine levels.

"Nitrous oxide system," Corbin yelled over the screaming engine. "It's a fucking blast!"

Fear thudded through Saengkeo as she saw how close they were to the staggered line of traffic. If someone chose to pull out onto the shoulder, there was no way the woman could stop the big vehicle in time.

Gradually the NOS leaned out and the Suburban's speed returned to normal. A glance over Saengkeo's shoulder showed her that the motorcycles had faded in the distance.

"Why are you here?" Kwan asked from the back seat.

"You mean, other than to save your ass?" Corbin asked.

"Yes."

The woman turned her attention to Saengkeo. "I wanted to get a look at you up close and personal. Check out the competition. See what was what." She lit another cigarette and exhaled through the partially opened window. The slipstream sucked the smoke away. "I've known Rance Stoddard for a few years now, but I've never seen him so interested in a source before. I wanted to see what made you so different."

"If you're based in Hong Kong," Saengkeo said, "you've already seen me."

"I'm there," Corbin replied. "I came in on the same flight you did. Didn't make first-class, though." She took a drag on the cigarette. "I have to admit, I'm kind of disappointed that I had to save you." She slowed the Suburban to pull onto Highway 110 and turned southbound. "Especially with the inscrutable Johnny Kwan along for the ride."

Suddenly two cars sped up from the traffic merging from 110. One of them pulled in front of the Suburban and the other snugged in close on the driver's side.

Corbin glanced at the vehicles. Before she could turn her head back, Kwan shoved one of his pistols against her right temple.

"Pull the car over," Kwan ordered in English.

"And if I don't?" Corbin asked, making no move to do as she'd been told.

"Then I shoot you through the head," Kwan replied. "Even if Miss Zhao can't remove your body from the wheel, my men blocking this car will control it and keep it from racing into any other traffic."

Corbin flicked her gaze to the rearview mirror. "You figure you have this wired, don't you?"

"Yes," Kwan said.

"Gonna leave me alive?"

Kwan didn't answer.

"Yes," Saengkeo said. "If you're who you say you are, we won't track you down and kill you."

"Boy. Now, there's a bonus you don't see every day when you get into the hero biz." Corbin braked gently and pulled over onto the shoulder. "I'm pulling over, Kwan, because Miss Zhao said she'll let me live. I don't trust you, but I know you'll do what she says to do."

Kwan remained silent.

When the Suburban rolled to a stop, Saengkeo reached over and switched off the ignition. She took the keys.

"Leaving me stranded?" Corbin asked with a trace of belligerence.

"Leaving you alive," Saengkeo countered. "As you so eloquently pointed out, someone set me up."

"And I'm suspect?"

"Yes."

"Even after I pulled your ass out of the fire?"

"Especially after you pulled my ass out of the fire," Saengkeo assured the woman.

Unexpectedly Corbin smiled, then laughed out loud. "I like you, Miss Zhao. Try to stay alive. I'd like to talk again."

Saengkeo nodded and stepped from the Suburban. She walked to the closer car, knowing Johnny Kwan wouldn't quit the vehicle until she was safe. But he also wouldn't kill Jacy Corbin.

Seated in the back of the sedan in front of the Suburban, Saengkeo dropped the MAC-10 into the seat beside her and let out a long, shuddering breath. She watched the traffic flowing beside her as the driver eased into the flow. Harsh white lights glared behind her, and before her stretched a seemingly endless river of red taillights.

Jacy Corbin, if that was the woman's name, was right about one thing, Saengkeo knew. She had been set up and marked for death. But did that have something to do with Wai-Lim Yang and the Black Swans or one of the other triads she'd offended in Hong Kong only a few days ago, or was it part of whatever secrets had killed her brother?

She forced herself to relax. She was only minutes away from Pei-Ling. Perhaps part of the mystery would be cleared up then. Knowing who was responsible wouldn't make her enemies go away, but Saengkeo knew she would feel better once she knew who the target was.

Still, the man in black remained, as did the missing nuclear weapons Rance Stoddard had her searching for.

Hong Kong

RANCE STODDARD GLARED at the monitor view afforded through the satellite relay sending images back from Los Angeles. The magnification of the scene was excellent, but due to the top view of the situation, he couldn't see inside the black Suburban Johnny Kwan was only now stepping down from.

"Who were the attackers?" Stoddard asked.

Kelso glanced at his computer screens. He'd already tied into the LAPD systems. "The officers arriving on the scene have tentatively identified the dead men as Steel Tigers."

Stoddard raised an inquiring brow.

"Local Asian gang of triad wanna-bes," Kelso said. "They've got a hefty file with the LAPD."

"Any usual contacts among the triads?"

"They do carjacking," Kelso replied. "Carjacking means

they eventually do business with United Bamboo even if that business is four or five times removed."

"Do they have a sponsor among United Bamboo?"

"No."

"That's in the file?" Stoddard asked.

"Yes."

"Do we have someone in the LAPD ACTF that can verify what those members have been doing lately?"

"I'll find one," Kelso promised.

Stoddard rested his elbows on the chair's armrests, then steepled his fingers together to support his chin. On the monitor, Kwan climbed into one of the cars that had blocked the Suburban off Highway 110. He was surprised to see the vehicle sitting there. He wondered if Kwan had killed the driver.

At first he'd thought that the Suburban had been part of Kwan's backup plan. Then when he'd seen the standoff that had obviously taken place between Kwan, Saengkeo and whoever the driver was, he had known that hadn't been the case.

So who would buy into the trouble that Saengkeo Zhao was in?

Stoddard had no answers.

Irritated, the CIA agent flicked his gaze to other monitors. Kelso had also tapped into a news feed from Vancouver, British Columbia, that was covering the explosions and running gun battles that had taken place in the building above the Nautilus Club.

The three CIA agents had been taken into custody by the local police force. Stoddard had already started working through diplomatic channels to see to their release. He was certain he would have them free and on the street again by morning local time.

There was no word of the mysterious man in black or his partner. From the way things looked, the two men had escaped without being apprehended.

"Hey," Kelso called. "I think we just found Jacy."

Intensely curious at once, Stoddard followed the other agent's gaze. There, on the screen that showed the action in Los Angeles, Jacy Corbin clambered out of the Suburban.

The female agent stood in a relaxed manner against the Suburban long enough to shake loose a cigarette and light up in her cupped hands. She breathed out a long plume of smoke and started walking southbound on 110.

"Contact our interface team," Stoddard said, his throat feeling slightly tight. "Have them cut the satellite links. We're done there for the moment."

Kelso nodded and bent to the task.

Stoddard watched the small figure of Jacy Corbin trudging alongside the highway. What the hell was she doing there? What did she think she knew?

A moment more and the screen turned black, leaving Stoddard alone with his questions and his increased worry. Things seemed on the verge of falling apart everywhere. He had to find the team that had interfered with the recovery of the nuclear weapon in the Indian Ocean, and then had chosen to move their front to Vancouver, British Columbia. Things were bad enough when Saengkeo Zhao had slipped away to have her meeting with Pei-Ling Bao, whom Stoddard had sincerely hoped would never be heard from again.

But now Jacy was out there among them.

Stoddard was grimly aware that he was captaining a small line of dominoes, and they were shaking in the breeze.

Vancouver, British Columbia

"SAENGKEO ZHAO HIRED me to spy on Eric Barnes."

Seated across from De-Ying Wu in the warehouse space along the docks Barbara Price had directed them to, Bolan studied the woman in the light of a small desk lamp. The assault on Eric Barnes had ended more than an hour earlier. Escaping undetected from the building hadn't been easy, but the effort had proved possible. They had walked to the SUV Bolan had cached three blocks away. Grimaldi had arrived at the Nautilus Club by cab.

Wu held a foam coffee cup in both hands. Steam drifted in the air in front of her face.

Bolan sat behind the desk in the second-floor loft space that overlooked the main warehouse space. The warehouse actually belonged to a thriving import-export business owned by shell companies owned in turn by the United States government. Stony Man Farm had access to the facilities, and the Executioner had chosen to use the warehouse as a temporary headquarters while he regrouped. Taking down Eric Barnes had only been the opening salvo of the assault against the Moon Shadow assets that he had planned.

"Why were you supposed to spy on Barnes?" Bolan asked.

Wu sipped at her coffee and shivered a little. The chill coming in across Burrard Inlet ghosted through the warehouse. Strong winds made the timbers creak as they battled to hold on to the corrugated metal.

"Because Saengkeo didn't trust him," Wu answered.

"Didn't trust him in what way?" Bolan pressed.

"She kept two different kinds of businesses in Vancouver."

When he realized that Wu wasn't going to open herself up any further, Bolan said, "Legitimate businesses and illegitimate businesses."

"Yes."

"Barnes handled some of the drug trade she was doing."

"Saengkeo didn't like the drug trade," Wu said, "and Barnes handled a *lot* of the drug trade. He also handled the high-end clients. Movie and television people. Dealers that worked the party scene throughout Vancouver and moved more of the product into Canada's interior."

Bolan cut his glance at the LCD screen of the notebook

computer to his right on the desk. The other notebook computer, the one he'd taken from the people who'd captured Grimaldi, sat on the floor with the lid closed. The modem and hard drive lights flickered, showing the intense activity that churned through the phone connection as Price and Kurtzman battled through the computer's safeguards and attempted to download the information contained in the files.

The LCD screen Bolan looked at showed front and profile shots of De-Ying Wu on a split screen. A copy of her Seattle, Washington, private investigator's license occupied the top window.

"Do you make it a habit to work for criminals?" Bolan asked.

Wu gave him a severe glance. "Are we counting the questions I'm answering for you?"

Despite his battered features, Grimaldi smiled. He stood behind Wu, and she didn't see the expression. The pilot definitely wasn't going to be of much use in public situations because he stood out.

"Yeah," Bolan replied. "We are counting the questions I'm asking you."

"Because you aren't exactly angelic," Wu said.

Bolan waited.

"In fact," Wu said, "you haven't even mentioned who you are or who you're with. You come on like a couple of gangbangers, but you're hooked up like James Bond."

"Saengkeo Zhao," Bolan said.

"You've got a one-track mind."

Bolan didn't reply.

"You're not the police," Wu said. "If you had been, we'd have been at the police station by now."

"No. We're not."

"So what are you doing here?"

"Investigating," Bolan said. "Like you."

"No." Wu shook her head. "You aren't anything like me. You're something way more...dangerous. I shouldn't even be here with you."

"You didn't have to be."

Wu raised a skeptical eyebrow. "I had a choice?"

"Yeah."

"Nobody saw fit to mention that on the way over here."

"You didn't exactly kick and scream," Grimaldi pointed out. "So why are you here?"

"To protect my client," Wu answered. "And to protect myself. Getting busted by the Vancouver cops would have been detrimental to my assignment and my career." She pointed to the white bags on the desk. "The offer still good on the sandwiches?"

Bolan pushed over the bags. After leaving the Nautilus Club and dropping Bolan at the warehouse, Grimaldi had gone for food. The night was going to be a long one.

Wu put down her coffee and rummaged through the bags. She took out a sandwich wrapped in wax paper, and a small container of potato salad. She folded the paper back and took a bite with strong white teeth.

Bolan sipped his own coffee and watched the woman with interest. Barbara Price and the Stony Man Farm intelligence-gathering teams had worked up a full background check on De-Ying Wu. The private investigator was thirty-two years old and had been on her own for the past six years after putting in time on the Seattle PD, ending up working the Asian Task Force. Her partner's death had caused her to turn in her shield and weapon, choosing to become a single operative. She specialized in skip-tracing and background checks for the electronics developers in and around the Seattle area.

"Why did Saengkeo hire you?" Bolan asked.

Wu wiped her lips with a napkin. "That comes under detective-client privileged information."

"Maybe not," Bolan said.

"You can't make me talk."

Bolan didn't make a response, letting her words hang in the still, musty air between them.

Wu glanced at Grimaldi for support. With his battered features, the pilot didn't look awe-inspiring or even much in the way of sympathetic.

"Don't give me the tough, silent act," Wu said.

"I can have your license revoked," Bolan told her.

Agitation darkened Wu's features. "Who are you people?"

"Someone who's serious about getting to know more about Saengkeo Zhao."

"Why?"

Bolan shook his head.

"I don't believe you," Wu said.

In the next instant, the image of the private investigator's license went up in flames on the notebook computer's LCD screen. The image had an effect on Wu, and the action let the woman know that whoever was working the other end of the computer connection was listening in.

"Believe," Bolan said. He hated leveraging the information from the woman the way he was, but things in Vancouver with Saengkeo Zhao's Moon Shadow operations felt off.

"What are you?" Wu demanded. "CIA?"

Bolan sipped his coffee. "Why did you agree to work for Saengkeo Zhao?"

Wu grimaced. "Because she asked, and because I knew the money would be good. I hadn't counted on tipping myself off to Eric Barnes's goon squad."

"How did that happen?"

"I was shadowing his operations, watching how he moved the drugs around, saw who he was dealing with."

"Did you find out much?"

Turning her attention to her sandwich, Wu took a bite,

chewed and swallowed. "Barnes was skimming and dealing off the books. Saengkeo knew that and wasn't worried about it. She was still turning a profit. However, what she wanted to know was whether Barnes was endangering her other businesses."

"Which businesses?" Bolan asked.

"The legitimate ones."

"How?"

"Barnes was shipping drugs through the legitimate shipping lines. He'd gotten people hired onto the operations and got them to ship the drugs. Saengkeo didn't want the legitimate businesses endangered."

"Why?"

"Because she didn't want to see the people running them get hurt or get involved with criminal activity."

Bolan turned that over but didn't feel convinced. The feeling had to have shown.

"How much do you know about Saengkeo Zhao and the Moon Shadow triad?" Wu asked.

"They're a struggling crime family that goes back two hundred years. They're involved in gambling, prostitution, smuggling, drugs and supporting street gangs that do carjackings, robbery and kidnapping."

"Your information is wrong," Wu said. "The carjackings, robberies and kidnappings are attributed to the Moon Shadows, but they're actually done by street gangs claiming affiliation with the Zhao family. The Moon Shadows have stayed away from personal-injury crimes for years."

"What about the drugs, the prostitution and the gambling?"

"Talk to some of the justice system proponents out there," Wu suggested. "A number of people believe those are victimless crimes. Only people who would involve themselves in those pursuits somewhere else are serviced. Nobody makes anyone use drugs, gamble or sell their bodies, and cases can be made against the legitimate ways companies, corporations and individuals have found around the law. But the Moon Shadows haven't set themselves up as thieves. The only protection they offer to shopkeepers is real, to keep other triad families or street gangs from preying on them."

Bolan made a mental note. "None of that came up in the information I've had access to." He knew his statement would set Price and Kurtzman scurrying through the cybernetic battlefields to track down the truth of the statement.

"That's not surprising," Wu said. "A lot of criminal activity gets pinned on the Moon Shadows. But if you go down into the Chinese communities and talk to the warlords and the shakers and movers in the crime scene, you'll find that everyone there has the same opinion that I do."

"The Moon Shadows don't exactly belong to a nonprofit organization," Grimaldi said. He stepped forward and took up one of the sandwiches from the bag himself.

"No," Wu agreed. "And I would never make that claim. The worst thing anyone can do is harm someone protected by the Moon Shadows. But the Zhao family doesn't live solely on the pain and suffering of others. Check with any ACTF member who has had dealings with the Moon Shadows and you'll get the same assessment nearly every time."

Then why was Saengkeo Zhao so interested in the nuclear weapons that went missing from *Kursk?* the soldier asked himself. And how coincidental was it that her brother was murdered the morning after the night the weapons all went missing from a Russian *mafiya* ship bound for a deal set up with Middle Eastern terrorists?

Bolan changed the subject. Wu obviously believed what she was saying. He had to dig more deeply, keep applying pressure until something broke loose.

"So you went to work for Saengkeo Zhao for the money?" he asked.

"You're pretty damn judgmental, aren't you?" Wu countered.

Bolan let the comment pass.

"I went to work for Saengkeo Zhao," Wu went on, "because she convinced me there were a lot of innocent people she was trying to protect, people she was trying to help build better lives here in North America. If Eric Barnes had gotten caught using her legitimate businesses the way he was, those people stood to lose everything. Including their freedom. Do you know how China feels about people who leave them?"

Bolan knew, but he didn't say.

"Do you know what a snakehead is?" Wu asked.

"Yeah," Bolan said. "A person that traffics in illegal aliens."

"Right. Snakeheads gouge Chinese citizens, take their money every time they save it up and make them agree to work for years in virtual servitude in Canada or the United States to pay for their passages. Sometimes a whole family works to afford one member's release."

Bolan knew that.

"Chinese illegals who are caught and deported," Wu said, "would rather be executed than to be returned to China. They're declared enemies of the Communist state and sometimes killed by government soldiers as an example to others who might want to leave the country. Do you know what that does?"

"Drive the price the snakeheads can charge to illegals higher," Bolan said.

"Exactly. Saengkeo Zhao doesn't do that. Neither did her brother. Both of them worked to provide real citizenship opportunities and legitimate jobs to their family members."

"Why?" Grimaldi asked.

"Because the Zhao family wants out of the crime business," Wu said. "If you look at the activities they're involved in, the things they're investing their future and their money in, they're not interested in staying with a life of crime. They haven't been for decades."

"Who told you that?" Bolan asked.

"Saengkeo Zhao," Wu replied. "When she hired me."

"And you believed her?"

"Yes. You'd have had to talk to her yourself."

BOLAN SAT BEHIND the SUV's steering wheel thirty minutes later. He drove through the streets, his mind whirling with the night's activities and the plans he'd already put into motion.

Grimaldi sat in the next row of seats back. De-Ying Wu sat beside him, showing the effects of the long night.

Steering through the heavy night traffic, Bolan pulled into the temporary parking area of the Pan Pacific Hotel Vancouver. The hotel was located on the waterfront, offering a staggering view of the harbor and the coastal mountains.

De-Ying Wu had backup reservations at the hotel. Bolan felt confident that the woman also had plans to get herself back out of the country without attracting notice.

Grimaldi stepped out of the SUV and held the door for the woman.

Wu started to walk away, then turned and came back. She looked at Bolan through the passenger window. "I feel as though I should thank you for saving my life tonight, but I don't want to."

"Then don't," Bolan suggested.

"Okay," Wu said. "But instead of thanking you, I'll offer you a piece of advice."

Bolan waited.

"Don't plan on going up against Saengkeo Zhao or the Moon Shadows," Wu said. "If you do, she'll bury you."

Bolan held the private investigator's gaze for a moment.

"God, but you're stubborn," Wu said, a grimace forming on her face. "You're turning me loose, knowing I'm going to tell Saengkeo Zhao about you."

"I'd rather you didn't," Bolan replied.

"And you know I can't not mention it." Wu's face hardened. "Whatever set you onto the Moon Shadows' trail, I damn sure hope it's worth it."

"Take care of yourself," Bolan said. "Saengkeo Zhao may not be exactly the positive force that you think she is."

"I'd rather die with my mistakes than live in fear of making them." Without another word, Wu turned and walked into the luxurious hotel.

Grimaldi opened the passenger door and clambered up into the seat. Bolan put his foot on the accelerator and found his way back out onto the street.

"She believes what she's saying, you know," the pilot said. His voice sounded strained because of all the swelling to his face.

"I know," Bolan replied. The neon lights of the downtown businesses around him reflected off the SUV's windshield.

"Some of what she said could be true," Grimaldi said.

"Yeah."

"So what are you going to do?"

"Try to put pressure on the Moon Shadows triad," Bolan answered. "Just like I came up here to do. This mission isn't wrapped until those missing nuclear weapons are found and safely recovered. Right now, Saengkeo Zhao and the Moon Shadows are the only lead I can work on."

11

Los Angeles, California

"Oh, Saengkeo! I had started to think that perhaps you weren't coming after all."

Saengkeo stood her ground as Pei-Ling Bao raced across the luxurious room toward her with open arms. Although she was in her early thirties, only a year younger than Saengkeo, Pei-Ling had never given up acting like a girl. The other woman hugged Saengkeo fiercely, causing renewed aches and pains to fill her body.

"I told you I would be here," Saengkeo said. She patted the other woman on the back, enduring her embrace but wishing she still had the innocence of the friendship they'd shared in their youth. Since Pei-Ling had grown aware of the interest shown her by men, that innocence had been lost.

Pei-Ling held on to Saengkeo's upper arms and took a step back. Tears sparkled in Pei-Ling's eyes; enough to make her eyes shine, but not enough to ruin the makeup she'd laboriously applied. Whatever had happened to Pei-Ling during the days that she had been abducted, none of the marks showed.

"I'm so sorry about Syn-Tek," Pei-Ling said. She looked genuinely distressed.

Maybe she even was, Saengkeo thought guiltily. However, Syn-Tek had made it evident from their teenage years when Pei-Ling had started to follow in her mother's footsteps that he didn't approve of her. Pei-Ling hadn't been approving of Syn-Tek, either, always pointing out his faults to Saengkeo. Syn-Tek, Pei-Ling had always insisted, was much too serious and didn't know how to have fun.

That disapproval extended to Johnny Kwan, who had never cared for Pei-Ling. He had never been offensive about his dislike, but it had been a constant and apparent thing. Kwan stood in the corner of the room, supervising the setup of the additional televisions and security devices that his teams would have in place in minutes.

"Thank you," Saengkeo said.

"You don't have to thank me," Pei-Ling replied, dismissing the effort with a wave of her hand. "I thank you for coming to get me, and for having the attorneys intercede on my behalf."

"Pei-Ling, we need to talk."

"I know, I know." Pei-Ling turned and walked away to the center of the room. She put her hands on her hips and looked sorrowful. In her own way, she was a beautiful woman, and she knew how to wear a room as well as the garments she had selected.

She wore her dark hair piled on her head. Her figure was full, designed to catch the eyes of men, and the dark blue lounging pajamas she wore showed off that figure to her best advantage. What nature and exercise had not given her, she had purchased from plastic surgeons.

She sighed dramatically and pushed out her breath. "There

is just so much to tell you. Can we go outside? There is a beautiful view of the harbor here, and nighttime in this city is breathtaking. I'd forgotten what L.A. looked like. I didn't know I had missed being here so much."

It had been years since Pei-Ling had been to L.A. That had been back during her porno video days, back when she'd been certain the American X-rated films producers would have more to offer her than the Chinese triad producers. Pei-Ling had ended up making dozens of movies in less than a year, becoming something of a sensation.

"Outside is not safe," Saengkeo said.

"I want to go out there," Pei-Ling said as petulantly as a child, then glared at one of Kwan's security team. "But they won't let me."

"The last time you were here," Saengkeo said, "things were very dangerous."

"I know." Pei-Ling looked sad. "I still miss him, you know. I loved him very much."

During her last tour of L.A., Pei-Ling had ended up involved with Terence Yip, one of the rising stars in United Bamboo that at the time had handled corporate espionage and drug trafficking in the metro area. Yip had been executed by one of the street gangs that was losing its territory to Yip's encroaching supply.

At the time, Pei-Ling had been implicated in setting up Yip's assassination. There were some among the United Bamboo triad who still believed that Pei-Ling had taken money to get Yip alone and vulnerable. Saengkeo had been forced to ask her father to intercede on her friend's behalf against the other triad families and the United States law-enforcement people, and there had been considerable expense for lawyers, as well.

"We can't go outside, Pei-Ling," Saengkeo said. The town house she had rented was on the harbor proper and policed heavily by local security. She waved to the breakfast nook in the far corner of the room. "Let's sit there while we talk."

Pei-Ling grimaced like a small child being asked to do something she didn't want to do. But after a quick glance at Saengkeo, she retreated to the small glass-topped table and chairs. Her hips rolled beneath the blue silk of her lounging pajamas, drawing the attention of every man in the room, except for, perhaps, Johnny Kwan.

A tea service had been laid out on the table. Saengkeo checked the pot with her hand and found it still warm.

"The tea is fresh," Pei-Ling said. "The people you have assigned here have taken very good care of me."

"Good." Saengkeo sat. She poured tea, then added lemon.

Pei-Ling generously added cream and sugar to her tea. Her metabolism helped keep her voluptuous rather than fat. But Saengkeo knew that even that metabolism would fail her friend at some point, as it had failed her mother before her. Pei-Ling would never have the willpower to save herself. Saengkeo forced the thought out of her mind.

"You were with the Soaring Dragons when you were recovered," Saengkeo said.

"Yes." Pei-Ling shuddered and wrapped her arms around herself theatrically. "It was horrible. They raped me. Not once, but several times. They were dogs."

With her friend's background in prostitution, Saengkeo knew Pei-Ling had slept with all kinds of men. The only difference between those men and the Soaring Dragons had been that Pei-Ling had gotten paid. Still, every time Saengkeo looked at her friend, she didn't think of the prostitute; she thought of the young, frail and terrified girl she had been.

"Those Soaring Dragons are dead," Saengkeo said.

"I know. But perhaps some of them escaped. I wouldn't want any of the men who were involved with that to get away. They need to be punished for what they did."

"I have people looking into that," Saengkeo said. She did, but she didn't plan to do much about it. Pei-Ling hadn't been an innocent in a long time. "Tell me about the man who rescued you."

Pei-Ling let go her arms and lights danced in her eyes. She smiled. "He was magnificent, Saengkeo. You should have seen him."

Saengkeo knew that she possibly already had, but she refrained from commenting.

"At first, I had thought that you had sent an army after me, Saengkeo," Pei-Ling said. "I knew that you would do that."

"I didn't know where you were."

Pei-Ling shrugged. "If you had known, you would have sent an army. I know you would have." She captured Saengkeo's hand in hers. "You have always been my friend. Even when other people turned away from me, you were always my friend." She pulled Saengkeo's hand against her cheek. "I love you for that."

Saengkeo noticed Kwan's brief flickering look of disgust but chose to ignore it. "Do you know who the man was?"

"No," Pei-Ling said, releasing Saengkeo's hand. "He was American, though. You could hear it in his voice. He talked as the Americans do." She drew her legs up onto the chair and wrapped her arms around her knees. She was a little girl again, talking privately with her friend but putting on a show for Kwan and the other men. The blue silk pajamas molded to the curves of her flanks.

"Did he tell you his name?"

"No." Pei-Ling's eyes glowed more brightly. "But you should have seen him. Every time he moved, one of the Soaring Dragons died." Putting her hands together, forefingers and thumbs outstretched and touching, the other fingers rolled in toward her palms, she mimed shooting a pistol. "I didn't know how one man could stand up to so many foes and emerge alive, let alone victorious." She sent a scathing look in Kwan's direction. "Until that day, I had thought only Johnny Kwan capable of a trick like that."

Saengkeo resisted the impulse to tell Pei-Ling that such a thing was no trick, that men had died. But Pei-Ling would have been vindictive about the deaths, and she wouldn't have understood the risk anyway. Pei-Ling only understood that someone had killed for her, and had risked death himself.

"This man," Pei-Ling said, "this man was like one of the magnificent warriors you and I used to dream about as girls."

Actually, Saengkeo had never dreamed of such a man. She had grown up around her father, her brother and Johnny Kwan. She had already know what such men were like, the prices they paid, as well as mistakes they were capable of making and the failings they were capable of having.

"Was he one of the Border Patrol or the INS?" Saengkeo asked.

Pei-Ling's brow wrinkled as if she were giving the question great thought. The effort was an act, designed solely to bring more attention to herself. "I don't think so. I've seen those men before. None of them act as quickly and as certainly as this man did. He was death, Saengkeo. I mean that. I've never said that about a man before. But this one was death." Her eyes lost focus, and Saengkeo was certain she was remembering the battle.

For a moment Saengkeo was distracted, remembering the brief but violent battle aboard *Charity's Smile*.

"No one was with him?" Saengkeo asked.

Pei-Ling shook her head. "No one. He was alone then."

Saengkeo remembered the pictures that had been broadcast across the American news services. Her information teams had gathered video files, as well as newspaper photographs. Other video from passing motorists with camcorders had been contacted and copies had been purchased. The site had been a battlefield, with bodies and wrecked vehicles scattered for miles. There had been a number of Border Patrol guards killed and injured.

But one man had made it through that firestorm and killed the Soaring Dragons while rescuing the hostages.

"It was amazing," Pei-Ling said, echoing Saengkeo's thoughts.

"Afterward," Saengkeo asked, "was this man joined by anyone?"

"No."

Saengkeo thought about that. In the Indian Ocean there had been another man, a pilot.

"Nor was there anyone when we went to the motel room later," Pei-Ling said in a casual manner.

Saengkeo looked at her friend sharply. "What motel room?"

"He took me to a motel room after he helped me escape."

"You were not wounded."

Pei-Ling shook her head. "No."

"Then why did he take you?"

"He wanted to talk to me."

"He knew you were there?"

"Yes." Pei-Ling looked proud. "He came looking for me."

"Why?"

Shrugging, Pei-Ling said, "I don't know."

"Did he tell you his name?"

"No."

"What did you do there?"

"He asked me questions."

Irritation chafed Saengkeo. Only Pei-Ling would forget that someone had questioned her in such a manner. "What questions?"

"About the Moon Shadows."

Kwan's head came around quickly and focused on Pei-

Ling. The woman cringed a little, glancing quickly at Kwan, then away. It was one thing to suffer Kwan's avoidance, but quite another to suffer his disapproval.

"What did he ask you about my family?" Saengkeo asked.

"He just wanted to know...things."

"What things?"

Pei-Ling shrugged helplessly. "I don't know. *Things.*"

Kwan crossed the room and was at Pei-Ling's side in an eye blink. "You are a silly girl." He gripped her wrist with bruising force and halfway yanked her from the chair. "What did you tell this man?" The ebony lenses of his sunglasses held twin images of Pei-Ling crouched in pain, her mouth open and her eyes closed in silent anguish and shocked disbelief.

Then the dam of emotions and frustration broke and Pei-Ling began to cry.

"Johnny," Saengkeo said, sitting quietly across the table. But she noticed that she'd waited until Kwan had totally terrified Pei-Ling, took away all hope of controlling the situation herself. Just a short time ago, Saengkeo would never have allowed such a thing to happen. But that had been before Syn-Tek had been murdered, before she had been forced to become the head of her family. She didn't know if she still possessed the luxury of a friendship...or even of mercy.

Kwan's nostrils flared as he breathed out. Still, his hand was steady as he opened his fingers and released Pei-Ling's wrist. He took two short steps back, just far enough to be out of instant reach, but he remained a constant looming threat.

And they all knew that Saengkeo had waited the studied fraction of a moment before calling him down.

Pei-Ling massaged her wrist and tucked her chin to her chest. Tears cascaded down her face. She shook with the effort of crying silently. In that moment she looked like the small, sad child she had been.

"Pei-Ling," Saengkeo said.

She shook her head. Then she got up as if to leave the chair. Johnny Kwan stepped in front of her, blocking her path but not touching her. Pei-Ling glanced at Saengkeo.

Saengkeo remained seated and didn't say anything.

Like a child, Pei-Ling stamped her foot, then sat back in the chair with her arms folded across her breasts. She tried to make her face hard and still, but her cheeks quivered.

"What did you tell this man?" Saengkeo prompted.

"Nothing!" Pei-Ling exploded. "There is nothing to tell, Saengkeo! He knew more about you and the Moon Shadows than I do! I don't belong to your precious family! Tonight, you have proved that to me! And Syn-Tek proved that when he sold me to the Soaring Dragons!"

Saengkeo felt as if she'd been hit with a sledgehammer.

Vancouver, British Columbia

BOLAN ARRIVED at Sports Fan Bar & Grill four minutes before midnight. He wore a long duster over the blacksuit. The .44 Magnum Desert Eagle rode his right hip, and the Beretta 93-R was snugged under his right arm. A shoulder sling held a Mossberg 500 Cruiser 12-gauge shotgun with a pistol grip. Kevlar covered the soldier's upper body, blunted and hidden by the loose folds of the duster.

A light mist mixed with fog rolled in from Burrard Inlet. The neon lights of the Sports Fan Bar & Grill gleamed against the rain-slick streets. Passing cars hissed through the rain as Bolan got out of his rental car and strode across the street.

The Sports Fan Bar & Grill was a semilegal business owned by the Moon Shadow triad. Price and Kurtzman had uncovered that fact. In addition to offering viewing on big-screen TVs, drinks and a limited menu with a mix of American and Chinese dishes, the club also ran a betting parlor on the second floor, as well as a sports book in the back.

The club wasn't one of the Moon Shadow triad's most lucrative institutions, but it was a place to start rattling cages. Situated only a short distance from the docks and the downtown area, the Sports Fan Bar & Grill took up the whole first floor in a wide-open pit filled with tables, pool tables, TVs and scantily clad servers.

Big windows allowed a good view of the bar area. Several people sat at the bar in the center of the room. Men and women bartenders, all Chinese, kept the drinks flowing as cash filled the registers and credit cards zipped through the readers. The service wasn't flashy, but it was steady. Televisions attached to the walls near the ceiling by boom arms offered views of recorded baseball games and ESPN.

Bolan stepped through the front door and kept moving. A slim young woman with blond hair met him.

"May I help you, sir?" Her accent was British.

"I know the way," Bolan said, turning toward the wide stairs to the left of the bar.

"I'm sorry, sir," the woman went on. "That area is off-limits after ten o'clock to all but guests. If you've been here before, you'll remember that."

Bolan didn't break stride. He felt the eyes of the bartenders and some of the clientele on him—only the clientele taking up space in the bar area weren't simply patrons. The intel packet had revealed that.

"Sir!" the woman called out. "I'll be forced to get security!"

"I'll want to see them, too," Bolan said gruffly.

One of the young men vaulted the bar. He wore a long-sleeved white shirt, black pants and a crimson vest. His clothing still left a lot of places to hide weapons. Two of the men in the back stood. Both of them wore sports coats.

"Sir," the bartender called out. He was young. A Fu Manchu mustache split the roundness of his baby face. He reached for Bolan.

Before the man's hands reached him, Bolan drew the Desert Eagle in one smooth move and pushed the barrel into the center of the man's forehead.

The man spread his hands and froze.

To the left of the stairway, the two men clawed under their jackets and came out with pistols.

Spinning, never losing sight of the bartender, the Executioner pointed the .44 Magnum pistol at the man on the right and fired twice from the point. Both heavy rounds caught the man in the chest and yanked him from his feet. Crimson blossomed across his white shirt.

Before the gunner landed on the floor, the Executioner had his partner in his sights and fired again. The bullet caught the second man in the shoulder and spun him, knocking the pistol from his hand.

The bartender launched a kick at Bolan's face. The soldier sidestepped smoothly, raised his left arm to block the kick and swept the Desert Eagle's heavy barrel alongside the bartender's head. The dulled thump of metal meeting flesh reached Bolan's ears even through the ringing echoes of the gunfire. Robbed of his senses, the bartender dropped in a loose-limbed heap to the floor.

The female server with the British accent started to scream and covered her head with her arms.

"Get down," Bolan ordered, shoving the woman to the floor where she would be out of the line of fire.

The gunshots started a stampede for the door. The patrons left in a hurry, overturning tables and chairs.

An alarm screamed, and Bolan knew one of the employees had triggered the warning. He'd guessed that he wouldn't get far into the building before the wheels came off the strike.

The Moon Shadow operation was tightly run, protecting itself from the local police department through vigilance.

Turning back to the stairs, Bolan saw the wounded man rolling over, the pistol once more in his hand. The man remained on the floor, rolling onto his side and bringing up the weapon.

Bolan took aim and fired, snapping the man's head back with a round. Two other men had kicked over tables and unlimbered weapons.

The Executioner holstered the Desert Eagle and sprinted toward the stairs, his boots ringing on the steel steps. Bullets struck the railing in showers of sparks. He grabbed the Mossberg's pistol grip and swung up the shotgun. He remained at a run, the numbers clicking steadily through his mind. The intel from Stony Man Farm had included blueprints and layout of the building.

At the top of the stairs, Bolan swept his gaze around. The front half of the second floor held video-game machines. Several of the screens were repixelating now, as if the power had been shut down, then switched back on. Bolan was sure that was the case.

The video-game machines in the Sports Fan Bar & Grill held a dual nature. On the surface, they were video games featuring player-controlled characters battling dragons, vampires and assorted enemies. But after hours, when the club enforced its members-only rule, those video game machines became video-lottery terminals hooked into the Internet that allowed casino-style gambling. Cash at the hidden offices turned into betting points on the machines. VLT machines had gotten to be problematic enough that the Chinese government had begun outlawing them in that country. Canada had become a primary location for them.

All of the machines were occupied. Most of the clientele stood one-on-one with the VLTs, but tourists grouped in couples and more stood at others. Most of them seemed frustrated with the sudden change in the video games. A few looked guilty or scared, obviously already familiar with what the alarm meant.

A hidden door opened in the wall to Bolan's right, behind two VLTs. The Executioner lifted the shotgun. Everyone in the upstairs section of the club stared at him.

The Chinese man who stepped from the hidden door raised an Uzi. Bolan swung the shotgun around and squeezed the trigger. The choked load of double-aught buckshot caught the gunner on the left side of his chest, blowing through his heart and ripping him around.

Screams penetrated the strident ringing of the alarms.

Bolan lifted his voice. "Out! Now!"

Hands over their heads, crouching in an effort to offer a smaller target, the gambling crowd rushed toward the stairs.

Catching movement at the top of the stairs from the corner of his eye, Bolan racked the shotgun's slide and spun. He fired at the man standing in profile to him, only his head and shoulders visible above the top step of the stairs.

The double-aught load caught the Moon Shadow gunner in the face and whipped him over the railing. The crowd rushed down the stairs.

Bolan thumbed fresh shells into the Mossberg and walked toward the hidden door left ajar.

A man threw himself from the doorway. Bolan's snapped shot cut the air a half step behind the man. Gunfire chattered through the room. Nine millimeter bullets slammed through the video-lottery terminals, blowing pieces of plastic and metal free. Sparks leaped from the gutted innards of the machines, followed by long, loose ropes of smoke.

Bolan whirled and dropped to one knee behind a terminal. He watched the man take cover behind another machine less than twenty feet away, duck out long enough to fire a dozen bullets, then pull back into cover. The Executioner racked the shotgun's slide and aimed for the VLT. When he pulled the trigger, the buckshot tore through the terminal's housing and hammered the gunman, knocking the man to the carpeted floor.

Thumbing more rounds into the Mossberg, Bolan watched as four men sped from the room and tried to take up positions in the hallway. The soldier remained merciless in his attack, racking the slide and pumping shells through the combat shotgun in a blur of motion. Double-aught buckshot filled the hallway. When the pellets didn't strike and tear flesh, they slashed the thin, modular walls to bits.

Bolan dropped the shotgun to his side, fed a fresh magazine into the Desert Eagle and drew the Beretta. Holding both pistols, the Executioner ran toward the hidden room. Movement of a video camera on the wall to his left drew his attention. Still on the run, he lifted the 93-R and put a round through the unit. Before the video camera debris had a chance to touch the floor, he fell into position beside the hidden room.

All five men in the hallway were dead.

Pistols up in both hands, Bolan swung around the door frame and dropped into a half crouch. He peered over the sights of the Desert Eagle and the Beretta at the three men in the room.

Two of them fired at Bolan. Bullets tore through the duster, and one struck him in the side but the Kevlar held. The blow still felt as if he'd been hit with an iron pipe and set off a wave of pain across his bruised ribs.

He squeezed the triggers, knocking down all three men in a hail of bullets. Combat senses alive, the Executioner stepped into the room.

Two of the men still lived, but the third had taken a round through the throat. Both survivors had been wounded. One of them looked as if he would live, and the other might make it if the paramedics arrived quickly enough and got him to a hospital.

Computer equipment filled the room, sitting on desks on both sides. A security camera station occupied the back wall. Video monitors showed the bar below, which was still in a state of confusion, and the smoking hulks of the destroyed video games on the second floor. Three of the screens were blank, evidently casualties of the attack.

One of the men reached for a pistol.

Bolan pointed the Desert Eagle at him. "Do it," the big man said coldly, "and you die."

After a brief hesitation, the man drew his hand back.

"English?" Bolan asked. He knew the security cameras were still operational. When the Vancouver police arrived, they'd find evidence of the gambling ring operation and put further pressure on the Moon Shadows. A war was all about the amounts and kinds of pressure a person could bring down on his enemies.

One of the men nodded. "Yes."

"Tell Saengkeo Zhao that she has lost this place," Bolan instructed.

"Yes." Hope dawned in the man's eyes that he would live.

"Tell her she knows why," Bolan went on.

"I will."

"Tell her that I won't stop until I have what I'm looking for."

The man nodded.

Gesturing with the pistols, Bolan got the men up and moving. He ordered them to go downstairs. Police sirens screamed in the distance. He knew from Price's intel that the on-site alarm system wasn't connected to the police station and guessed that one of the frightened clientele had called in. Or perhaps a nearby business. It didn't matter.

When the men were out of the room, the Executioner took a prepared C-4 charge from his combat harness. The explosive was small enough to do considerable damage inside a room but not cause any structural damage to the building. He set the five-second timer and tossed the C-4 into the midst of the video-game-room floor.

Bolan reached the midpoint of the steps, moving quickly now so he wouldn't be an easy target, when the explosive charge went off. The sudden flash of light stripped away most of the shadows in the bar area, the rolling wall of thunder erasing all other sounds.

The Executioner raced through the front door and crossed the street to the rental car, keying the electronic ignition and opening the door with the keypad. He slid into the seat, pulled the sedan into gear and sped down the street.

He gazed at the Sports Fan Bar & Grill in his rearview mirror. Smoke poured from the building's lower two floors. Small fires showed tongues of flame that reflected against the bar's windows and washed away the effect of the neon lights.

Eric Barnes had been a start, the soldier knew. But his plan was to rock and roll through the night, ramping up the stakes in the dangerous game he was playing against the Moon Shadow triad. He felt certain Saengkeo Zhao knew where the last remaining nuclear weapon was, and he intended to get the information.

He turned the corner and focused his thoughts on his next target. All of them were only minutes apart, and all of them were designed to strike critical blows against the Moon Shadow triad.

12

Los Angeles, California

"What did you say?" Saengkeo demanded. Surely she had heard Pei-Ling wrong. She stared at the woman seated across the table from her in the L.A. safehouse.

Pei-Ling drew back. Honest fear touched her face then, even more so than when Johnny Kwan had gripped her wrist.

"What did you say?" Saengkeo repeated.

Hesitation marked Pei-Ling's face, freezing her tears. "It's true, Saengkeo. Syn-Tek sold me to the Soaring Dragons."

"No." Saengkeo heard her response in her own ears and knew how weak her denial was.

"He did."

Saengkeo glanced at Johnny Kwan. She could read nothing from his face. "Did he?" she asked.

"Yes!" Pei-Ling said, rising from the chair and slamming her hand against the table hard enough to make their glasses jump. "Aren't you going to believe me? Saengkeo, you always knew when I was lying! You know I'm not lying now!"

Saengkeo ignored the other woman, keeping her attention focused on Kwan. What Pei-Ling had said was true: she never had been able to lie to Saengkeo. And if Pei-Ling was telling the truth... It couldn't be the truth. Saengkeo focused on that. Nothing else mattered.

"I don't know," Kwan stated flatly.

"How could you not know?" Saengkeo asked. Even though her brother was dead, she knew that Kwan would like to protect Syn-Tek's name even though he could no longer protect her brother.

"Because I was not involved," Kwan answered. "Nor were any of my men."

"Syn-Tek used other men," Pei-Ling insisted. "He didn't want any of you to know. Least of all you, Saengkeo. He knew how you feel about me."

"Why do you tell me that you don't know?" Saengkeo asked Kwan.

"Because," Kwan said, his voice devoid of emotion, "I had heard that Syn-Tek had hired the Howling Dogs to take Pei-Ling from Hong Kong."

Saengkeo knew of the Howling Dogs. They were one of the young street gangs in Hong Kong. Their petty thieving and gambling was allowed in Kowloon among the tourists. Of course, they also had to pay tribute to United Bamboo and the Big Circle Society for the privilege. The Howling Dogs would do anything for one of the larger triads.

"Why would Syn-Tek do this?" Saengkeo asked.

Kwan shook his head.

"Did you not ask?"

"No," Kwan answered simply.

Then Saengkeo remembered whom she was asking that question of. Kwan wouldn't ask. That fact was as certain as the sun's rising the next morning. Kwan wouldn't want the rumor to be true, nor would he want to know Syn-Tek's culpability in the matter. If Syn-Tek hadn't told Kwan, her brother hadn't intended that Kwan know.

Still feeling dazed, Saengkeo turned to Pei-Ling. She felt the anger at the young woman rise in her like an explosive napalm strike.

"It is true, Saengkeo!" Pei-Ling insisted in a voice loud enough to draw the uncomfortable attention of Kwan's men in the room.

"Why would Syn-Tek do this?" Saengkeo demanded.

Pei-Ling hesitated.

"What did you do?" Saengkeo asked.

"Nothing," Pei-Ling answered. "Why must it be I who did something wrong?"

"Because Syn-Tek would not do something wrong." At the same time that she said that, Saengkeo thought of the deal her brother had purportedly made with Rance Stoddard to get the nuclear weapons back that the Russian *mafiya* had stolen from the submarine. They'd had no reason to believe Stoddard or the CIA would upgrade their help in getting the Moon Shadows out of Hong Kong and into legitimate jobs in the Western world.

"Your brother," Pei-Ling said, "was not as perfect as you believe, Saengkeo."

Before she could stop herself, Saengkeo slapped Pei-Ling hard enough to turn her face. Saengkeo was instantly mortified at what she had done, but there was no taking the slap back.

Pei-Ling put her hand to her face. "Why did you do that?"

"Tell me what you did," Saengkeo said in a cold voice. All the unbridled rage she felt at Syn-Tek's mysterious death came bubbling up inside her, threatening to break loose.

"I never thought you would hit me, Saengkeo."

Saengkeo shut off the angry feelings, and she boxed away what little sympathy she had for Pei-Ling. "You will answer my questions."

"You are rude," Pei-Ling insisted.

Ignoring the accusation, Saengkeo said, "You will answer my questions or I will have Johnny Kwan ask them when I leave."

Real fear flooded Pei-Ling's face. "Are we not friends anymore?"

"Not if you had something to do with my brother's death."

"I didn't."

"Then tell me why Syn-Tek would sell you to the Howling Dogs."

Pei-Ling cried and sniffled. She was like a child who had been spanked by a parent who had never raised a hand against her. "I did nothing. I swear."

Saengkeo started to rise from her chair.

"The only thing I can remember," Pei-Ling went on, "before Syn-Tek came to my apartment with the Howling Dogs, was that I had seen him with a man."

Saengkeo's heart beat faster. Syn-Tek had been killed at close range. Her brother had known whoever had murdered him. And Syn-Tek had trusted him or her or them. Without warning, the image of the man in black with guns blazing filled her head. Or perhaps Syn-Tek had been killed by a man he had never seen coming.

"What man?" Saengkeo asked.

Pei-Ling resumed her petulance. "The CIA agent in Hong Kong."

"There are several CIA agents in Hong Kong."

Pei-Ling's brow wrinkled. "The chief one of them. Stoddard."

"You know Stoddard?"

Shrugging, Pei-Ling said, "Occasionally."

"How?"

The younger woman rolled her eyes. "As a client." Pei-Ling never called the men who slept with her for money johns or customers. That was beneath her, and beneath the services she provided.

"Stoddard appreciated your skills so much that he asked Syn-Tek to sell you to the Howling Dogs?"

"No. That was not how it was. Stoddard hasn't been a client in more than eight months."

"You remember?"

Pei-Ling waved the ability away. "I remember men, Saengkeo. That is how I make my money. I remember all the well-paying men."

"Or the men who can hurt you," Johnny Kwan said.

A little of the self-important pride fled Pei-Ling then. "Yes," she admitted.

"So you haven't seen Stoddard as a—" Saengkeo stumbled over the term "—a client in over eight months."

"No. Not since the new agent climbed into his bed. Her name is Jacy Corbin."

Saengkeo recognized the name immediately, but she had to wonder why Stoddard's lover would be in L.A. to save her.

"Did Stoddard talk to you that night?" Kwan asked.

Turning her attention back to the conversation, Saengkeo realized that Kwan had stepped in to ask the question that she should have been asking. However, the whole turn of events had made her feel as if the world had shifted treacherously beneath her feet.

"No," Pei-Ling answered. "But I don't think I was supposed to see them together. I didn't know Syn-Tek was working with the CIA."

"Where did you see them?" Saengkeo asked.

"In the harbor," Pei-Ling said. "They were on a boat together."

"Did Syn-Tek talk to you?"

"No. I was with another client. An American."

"What American?"

Pei-Ling waved the question away. "He was no one. A tourist I picked up in a bar. A doctor who had rented a boat and wanted a little action on the side when his wife wasn't looking."

Saengkeo's mind wrapped around the possibility that Syn-Tek would have sold Pei-Ling to the Howling Dogs. She had no doubt that her brother would have done that to protect the Moon Shadow triad's secret liaisons with the CIA. That secret was enough to get them all killed. Her stomach twisted sickeningly. Perhaps someone else had found out that knowledge and it had gotten her brother killed.

In fact, it was a miracle that Syn-Tek hadn't killed Pei-Ling out of hand. Sadness fluttered through Saengkeo when she realized that her brother had probably not killed Pei-Ling out of consideration for her, and that consideration may have been enough to get him killed.

"Did Syn-Tek talk to you the night he sold you to the Howling Dogs?" Saengkeo asked.

Pei-Ling shook her head. "He broke into my apartment with them. I asked him what he was doing, but he wouldn't speak to me. When one of the Howling Dogs shot me, I thought I was dead. Then I woke up on a ship a day or two later, I'm still not sure which. In South America somewhere, the Howling Dogs sold me to the Soaring Dragons."

Saengkeo remained quiet, digesting the unexpected information. Syn-Tek had kept so many secrets from her.

"You said the warrior in black asked you questions about the Moon Shadows," Kwan said.

Saengkeo refocused on the conversation with effort.

"Yes," Pei-Ling replied.

"He knew a lot about the Zhao family?"

"Yes. He had a computer. He showed me pictures of Saengkeo, Syn-Tek and you."

Saengkeo heard the vindictive note in Pei-Ling's voice

and knew that she was quietly taunting Kwan with the threat of the big man in black.

"No one else was with him?" Kwan asked.

"No, but he talked to someone on the phone."

"Who?"

Pei-Ling shrugged. "He never mentioned any names. As deadly as he was facing the Soaring Dragons, he was twice as careful around me." She looked at Saengkeo. "But he is very interested in you."

"Why?"

"I don't know."

"How did he find out about you?"

"I don't know."

Anxiety rattled through Saengkeo. There were so many things going on, and she had so few answers to dangerous situations.

One of the other men crossed the room and talked quietly to Kwan. Nodding, Kwan turned to Saengkeo. "There has been a problem."

"What?"

Kwan looked at Pei-Ling.

Saengkeo turned to the younger woman. "Go to your bedroom, Pei-Ling."

The woman looked as though she were going to argue for a moment. Then she got up haughtily and left the room. Saengkeo felt some of the tension leave her at Pei-Ling's departure.

"She is going to be difficult," Kwan predicted.

Saengkeo pinned the man with her gaze. "And what would you have me do? Sell her back to any surviving Soaring Dragons?"

Kwan didn't say anything, and in that silence Saengkeo knew that he would propose a final solution to the "difficulty" Pei-Ling posed.

"No," Saengkeo said. "For all her weaknesses and her flaws, Pei-Ling is still my friend."

Kwan nodded. "As you wish."

"What is the problem?"

"Eric Barnes has been killed in Vancouver," Kwan said.

Saengkeo couldn't say that she was truly surprised. She neither liked nor trusted Eric Barnes. Her brother, who had thought with his connections that he could move drugs for them more quickly to high-paying clientele, had pulled the man into the triad's business. Barnes had done exactly that. But he also skimmed money off the top, growing even braver in the days since Syn-Tek's death. Saengkeo had already hired private investigator De-Ying Wu to check into the matter.

"What happened?" Saengkeo asked.

"He was shot down, according to reports," Kwan said. "By a man dressed all in black." He pointed at one of the televisions against the wall. "Some of the film footage was captured."

"He's in Vancouver?" Saengkeo couldn't believe her luck, but she saw the blurred figure that could have been the same man in black that had been on *Charity's Smile.*

"Yes."

Suddenly, the world seemed a smaller place to Saengkeo. She heard the swirl of leaves in a graveyard whispering in her mind as she watched the warrior in black run through the hallways in the building.

Vancouver, British Columbia

THE APARTMENT BUILDING was located in Vancouver's West End, not far from Pendrell Suites, where many Hollywood movie and television stars stayed while filming in the city. Made of sleek glass and steel, the structure looked at home in the affluence of the city. The night poured around the building, flowing constantly.

Bolan left his car at the curb and walked to the covered entrance. The building looked elegant, a place that housed business offices or quiet private residences. The operation the Moon Shadow triad kept inside was quite different.

Several triad gangs in the Vancouver area kept "hot mattress" joints, places where Chinese women and women of other nationalities existed in virtual slavery to be used for sexual subjugation at a relatively cheap price. Vancouver vice police officers and undercover detectives found and raided such places on a somewhat regular basis.

But there were also a few upscale businesses that pandered to the sexual appetites for people ready, willing and able to pay for anything or anyone they fantasized about. The Moon Shadow triad owned the Carnation Building.

Only four stories tall and small, the Carnation Building's top two floors held expensive call girls in elegant suites. Those women serviced clientele and also did regular shows broadcasted over pay Web sites. Personalized photo shoots were also arranged, paid for over the Net and shipped by e-mail. Escort services and massage parlors filled the second floor.

The first floor offered business offices that supported the other facets of the operation, the billing, processing and verification of clients. The Web porn was legal in Canada, although the prostitution wasn't, and clients often masqueraded as "guests" starring on the Web cam shoots.

Getting a bust inside the building was difficult because the Moon Shadow operation carefully screened anyone who came through its doors. In addition, the first floor also offered city tours, a hairstyle salon and a travel agency, guaranteeing a reason for a lot of walk-in traffic so the police couldn't harass the customers by claiming to know why they were there.

The Carnation Building housed an efficient operation that was well protected.

Bolan stepped onto the red carpet under the canopied walkway. With the attack on the Sports Fan Bar & Grill, the soldier expected the security around the building to be increased. When he saw the two men lounging in the foyer behind the glass doors of the main entrance, he knew he was correct.

The doorman was Chinese, dressed in a white liveried suit with a blue carnation in the lapel. His eyes were flat and hard. From the way he kept his hand at his right hip, Bolan figured the guy had a pistol sheathed in a paddle holster at the small of his back.

"I'm sorry, sir," the man stated politely, taking a small step in front of Bolan. "The public offices are closed at this time of night."

"I know," Bolan said. "I've got an appointment." Velcro tabs closed the duster. He'd left the shotgun in the sedan so the duster masked the Kevlar, the .44 Magnum pistol and the Beretta 93-R.

"I can confirm that for you, sir." The man waved at the speaker box mounted on the wall. A security camera sat above the box.

"I can confirm it for you," Bolan offered. He took a wallet from his duster pocket and opened it to reveal the badge inside. The badge was an exact replica of the ones used by District One's West End Community Policing Center detectives. The accompanying photo ID even listed him as a vice department member.

"What's this about?"

"Maybe you'd better get a manager out here," Bolan suggested.

The man shook his head. "Not without a court order."

Bolan put away the badge and brought out a sheet of paper. Price and Kurtzman had been thorough. The court order was a legitimate-looking though false document.

The man scanned the page, then stepped back to the speaker box. He pressed a button. "I have a detective from vice at the front door. He's demanding entrance, and he has a court order."

Bolan waited. Simply walking into the building wasn't going to happen, and he wanted to do more than simple cursory damage to the operation. The Carnation Building's dealings remained viable only because customers trusted their discretion and their ability to protect them. Bolan intended to rip away that illusion tonight.

One of the two men inside the entrance answered a small handset radio from his jacket pocket. He nodded toward the other man, and they got up together.

Both men were slender and in their thirties. Their cold eyes and practiced movements, the way they spread out and kept from getting in the other's line of fire, revealed that they'd dealt with a number of similar situations.

"Who are you?" one of the new arrivals asked. Burn scarring that looked as if it were caused by lighted cigarettes marred his face.

Bolan showed the wallet and the court order again.

The man nodded.

Bolan put the document away.

"Why are you here, Detective?" the scar-faced man asked.

"Like the writ says," Bolan replied. "To search for any signs of prostitution on the premises."

The man smiled as if they were sharing a good joke. "Are you familiar with our business here?"

"No. I'm out of the Gastown District." Bolan went with the flow, trying to keep things easy for the moment. Penetrating the building was the most important thing.

"Perhaps someone is playing a joke on you."

Bolan hardened his voice. "That writ is no joke."

The man's smile went away. "No. Of course you are right."

He looked into the street behind Bolan. "But I am surprised that you came here alone."

"I was told I could do this myself," Bolan said.

"I see. Pardon me for a moment." The man stepped away and took the radio handset from his pocket again. He spoke rapidly in Chinese in a voice so low that Bolan couldn't overhear him.

"If you want," Bolan offered, "I'll make a call to the department and get a few of my colleagues down here. Of course, I'll be getting them out of bed. I can't guarantee their moods will be pleasant."

The man held up a hand and nodded. He finished with his conversation and put the radio away. "That won't be necessary, Detective. I only had to let the security office know that I would be bringing someone inside. They are very diligent in their job. Many things can happen in a city this size." He snapped his fingers at the other man.

The other security man stepped toward the door. An electronic lock popped and drew back from the door. He opened the door and stood politely back out of the way.

Bolan followed the scar-faced man into the building. The air-conditioning inside removed the thickness of the misty night outside and sent a chill along the soldier's neck.

"I am Mr. Qin. My associate is Mr. Bei," the scar-faced man said.

"You run security here?" Bolan asked. He stood in the foyer. The hallway extended in both directions. Two elevators, for the convenience of the guests, occupied the wall in front of the foyer opposite the main entrance. The carpet was blue and white, thick and expensive. Vases stood on pedestals or on the floor and contained a brilliant array of silk flowers. Paintings on the walls featured photos of the Vancouver sights, making the Carnation Building's community awareness and spirit apparent.

Qin smiled. "No. Where would you like to begin your...investigation?"

"The security offices," Bolan replied. "I'm sure I'm not going to see anything in the building that I can't see through the security monitors. Maybe I can make a short night of it for all of us."

"Of course. A short visit would be preferable for all concerned." Qin took the lead down the right hallway. His footsteps made no noise on the plush carpet.

Bolan followed, intensely aware that Bei had stepped in behind him. Around the next corner, Qin knocked on a small beige door marked Private.

Another electronic lock shot back. The door opened a moment later. A young Chinese man in a black suit stood framed there for a moment, looked at Bolan, then stepped back to allow entrance.

A thin man in his forties sat behind a small metal desk at the end of the room. He smoked an unfiltered cigarette that glowed briefly, reflected in the screen of the computer at his right. When he breathed out, the smoke wreathed his head. He stubbed out the cigarette with nicotine-yellowed fingers. The ashtray was nearly overflowing, mute testimony to the habit he had.

"Come in," the man said, waving Bolan in.

Bolan stepped inside the room.

Security monitors lined the wall to the soldier's right. Most of them showed women in various stages of undress in the middle of beds. The majority of the screens showed only one woman, but there were a few that had more than one woman. Fewer still had women working with male partners. All of them were engaged in sexual acts whether by hand, by latex objects or with each other.

"I am Mr. Hsiao," the man said. He didn't bother to rise from his chair. He shifted to look up better at Bolan. His coat flapped open, revealing, for the briefest moment, the pistol sheathed under his left arm.

Bolan nodded and introduced himself using the alias Price had set up. If the Moon Shadows ran a computer check on the name, that detective would indeed show up on the roster for the next few minutes. The Vancouver Police Department couldn't access that information from within their own systems, and only someone hacking into the employee files from off-site could reach that file.

"Do you have a permit for that weapon, Mr. Hsiao?" Bolan asked.

"Of course. All my men have such permits. Would you like to see them?"

"Yes."

Hsiao reached into the desk and brought out a thick record book. He pushed it across the desk to Bolan, turning the cover open and flipping to the section marked Weapons Permits. He revealed the pictures and permits of every man Bolan had seen so far.

"This isn't a dangerous part of the city," the Executioner said.

"No," Hsiao agreed. "And we do our part to keep it that way." Another small smile briefly flickered on his face.

Bolan was conscious of the two men standing behind him. He had no doubt that more men were already on call. He noticed the security camera behind Hsiao that offered a direct view of the door. The view, however, wasn't represented on the wall of security monitors offering views of the different bedrooms and massage parlors upstairs. The view was being transmitted somewhere else, but it remained to be seen where that was.

The gun permits looked in order. Bolan pushed the book back to Hsiao.

He turned his attention to the security monitors again. "That's a hell of a lot of activity," Bolan commented.

"Yes," Hsiao agreed. "But, as you can see for yourself, none of those activities are illegal in this city or province."

"Provided what I'm seeing is everything that's going on here," Bolan countered.

"Those women," Hsiao said with a knowing smile, "have precious little to hide. I think you will agree."

Before Bolan could reply, a shadow darkened the doorway.

A young man dressed in a black suit stepped into the room carrying a manila folder. He glanced at Bolan, then went for the pistol leathered beneath his jacket on his hip. The manila folder spilled from his hands, and a photograph slid out. As the photograph drifted toward the floor, Bolan yanked open his duster and reached for the Beretta 93-R under his right arm. He extended the silenced weapon as the photograph twisted and revealed a glossy shot of him striding through the Sports Fan Bar & Grill. Police wouldn't be able to identify the picture through records, but the image looked enough like him that the concern on the man's part was understandable.

In the situation he was in, deep inside enemy territory, Bolan knew he couldn't allow himself to be placed at gunpoint. He brought the 93-R up, firing as soon as he had target acquisition.

13

The first 9 mm Parabellum round sliced through the picture of Bolan as it drifted to the floor, then smashed into the man's right hip and corkscrewed the triad member around. The Executioner fired twice more, aware that the three other men in the room were going for their weapons. Both bullets struck the newcomer in the chest.

Turning, the soldier launched himself over Hsiao's desk. Bolan held the 93-R in his left hand and reached for the Chinese gangster with his right. He closed his right hand in Hsiao's shirt and bore them both down to the floor as bullets split the air over his head.

Gunshots rang out in the room.

Hsiao almost managed to get his pistol up, but Bolan shoved the 93-R under the man's chin and squeezed the trigger, twisting his head away from the sudden spray of blood. Hsiao shivered in his grip.

Rolling, combat senses on full alert, Bolan peered under

the desk and saw the men trying to back out of the room. He kicked his feet against the wall and shoved his way over Hsiao's corpse. Shooting out into the open on the other side of the desk, the Executioner levered the Beretta in front of him and squeezed the trigger rapidly.

His first three shots ripped through Qin's side, coring into his heart and lungs. His second set of three shots blasted into Bei's face, obliterating his features in a crimson rush.

Pushing himself to his feet, Bolan checked the computer on the desk and found the system was intact. He searched the menu and clicked on the Internet link. The machine booted up instantly. He pulled up a Web browser and typed in an address.

While he waited a handful of seconds for the link to be established, Bolan scanned the security monitors. None of the sex play on the screens was interrupted. Evidently the gunshots hadn't been heard and the rooms were soundproof.

The computer screen changed, fading to soft blue. Black letters declared "We're in."

"We" was Aaron Kurtzman and his specialized cybernetics team. The Web address had been set up for the night and was designed solely to feed all of the Carnation Building's files into the Stony Man Farm computer banks. Before reaching the Farm, though, the information would be juked along a system of cutouts that would make later computer forensic work on the part of law-enforcement teams impossible.

In the next instant, the monitor screen returned to its normal desktop, and the computer activity slid into the machine's background. At first glance no one would notice that the machine was processing.

Bolan drew the Desert Eagle and strode out into the hallway. He had already memorized the building's layout. He avoided the elevators. Wherever the secondary security office was that had access to the camera in Hsiao's office, the men staffing the place might be able to control the elevators.

No one was in the hall.

Bolan ran to the left, reaching the stairwell door in a dozen long strides. The door wasn't locked. He opened the door and started up the stairs, knowing he had little time.

Hong Kong

"TROUBLE."

Alert and agitated, Rance Stoddard glanced at David Kelso. "What?" Stoddard demanded.

"Our mystery guy is hot again," Kelso said, nodding toward the computer monitors in front of him.

Stoddard couldn't believe it. He had just been reviewing the damage the man in black had inflicted on the Sports Fan Bar & Grill little more than three hours ago. "Are you certain it's the same man?"

"If it's not," Kelso said, "then he's got a brother. A brother with the same moves. You tell me what the chances are of that."

Pushing himself up from his chair, Stoddard joined Kelso, standing back of the other man's seat. He watched as the man in black stepped through a doorway.

"Do we have sound?" Stoddard asked.

"Not on this patch," Kelso said.

Although they'd been able to tap most of the Moon Shadow triad's activities through the security network Syn-Tek had established, many of them only had video but not audio tracking. Stoddard knew that Syn-Tek Zhao had known of several of the taps.

Kelso tapped the computer keyboard. The monitors shifted, bringing the video camera in the building's stairwell to front and center.

"Still in Vancouver?" Stoddard asked.

Kelso nodded. "The Carnation Building."

"The whorehouse?"

"And the porno Web cam sites," Kelso added.

"This guy has a real hard-on for the Moon Shadows."

"This guy has a real hard-on for nuclear weapons," Kelso countered. "He just thinks the Moon Shadows know where they are."

Stoddard remained quiet, watching as the man in black moved from room to room. The man in black didn't harm any of the working women or their clients or "guests." A random thought occurred to the CIA section chief.

"Do we have a tap on the computer system there?" Stoddard asked.

"Yeah."

"Check it."

Kelso tapped keys, then paused. "It's live, too. Uploading like crazy."

"Someone's emptying the computer files," Stoddard said. He watched the man in black move from room to room. There was no wasted effort, and no mercy when he went up against the Moon Shadow security people. The triad shooters were anxious, and the male and female prostitutes were in fear for their lives. The rooms emptied quickly. Almost as quickly, Stoddard was certain, as the computer files.

"Why hit the computer?" Kelso asked. "It's not like the Zhao woman would keep the information there if she knew where the nukes were."

"For the same reason we tapped the computers and security systems," Stoddard said. "Information. It's the most valuable thing on this planet. He can't go to Saengkeo Zhao and make her tell him where the weapons are."

"He thinks she knows?"

"He must."

Onscreen, the man in black paused, dumping objects from his pockets to the floor of a room outfitted with a soundstage, a circular bed with satin sheets and torture equipment that would have looked at home in the Spanish Inquisition. Then he vanished through the next door.

Kelso lifted his hands to the keyboard.

"Stay with this room for a moment," Stoddard instructed.

Kelso left the view where it was, but he moved on through the security cameras, chasing the elusive man in black.

A moment later, the packages the man in black had scattered across the floor blew up. Stoddard had a brief impression of flames shooting out from the packages, then the cameras went dark.

"Explosives," Kelso commented.

"No shit," Stoddard replied.

"Guy's dealing scorched earth against the Moon Shadows."

"I know. You know who he reminds me of?"

"Us," Kelso said.

Stoddard nodded. "Run this guy up through the channels again. Get his face to every American espionage and law-enforcement agency you can."

"None of the pictures I've been able to download are very good," Kelso replied. "If we get a hit on this, I'll take you to Vegas."

"Do it," Stoddard ordered. "Dammit, this guy belongs to someone, and I want to know who. Then I want him out of my op."

"If he was agency issue somewhere along the way, he might not be now. He might be off the hook."

"Find out," Stoddard snapped. "If nobody wants to claim this son of a bitch, I want him taken off the board before he causes any more problems."

Without warning, the video feeds stopped. The screens went black.

Stoddard looked at Kelso.

"I got jammed up," Kelso explained. "Whoever is uploading the Carnation Building's files found out I was there and spiked me."

"Did you get anything?"

"Offended," Kelso answered. "They shook off the built-in programming like it was water off a duck's back."

"Did they find you?"

Kelso hesitated, then shrugged. "I don't know. I don't think so." He tapped the keyboard. "I'm shutting down access from that part of the world for a while. The way this guy is moving, we'll know where he's been and we'll know what he's done."

Remembering the professional way that the man in black had moved throughout the Carnation Building and the Nautilus Club before that, as well as the attack on *Charity's Smile,* Stoddard didn't doubt that. His stomach rolled menacingly, and he tasted sour bile at the back of his throat.

Too many things had gone wrong with the operation so far. Syn-Tek had been in good with the triads and had been moving into a position of power among them. Then he'd gotten himself killed. Saengkeo wasn't nearly as tractable as her brother had been. And Jacy Corbin was on her way to becoming a liability if she didn't pull back within the ranks.

Stoddard stared at the frozen image of the man in black on the footage he'd earlier been watching of the Nautilus Club. "Find him. Let me know who owns him. If they won't pull this guy in, we'll do it for them."

Vancouver, British Columbia, 1:47 a.m.

BOLAN PUSHED his glove back over his watch, erasing the telltale glow of the luminescent hands. He sat behind the wheel of a 4WD Ford Explorer that Price had arranged for.

The radio station he was tuned to carried live coverage of the "accident" at the Carnation Building an hour and a half earlier.

Police and fire department units still maintained a cordoned-off area around the building. So far there were no real details, other than several people were dead and that at least one man with automatic weapons had attacked the building personnel. The fires in the building were under control and were thought to be extinguished. The damage was going to be extensive.

Bolan reached for the foam cup of coffee on the dash and took a sip. He ignored the fact that he had sat hidden in the alley long enough for the liquid to cool. Fatigue gnawed at his reserves. He had one more item on his hit list before he called it a night and waited to see what Saengkeo Zhao's response would be.

"Striker," Price called over the headset he wore.

"Go," Bolan said. He poured the dregs of the coffee out the window, then threw the cup into a nearby garbage bin. He started the engine with a twist of the key.

"Your target is in motion."

Bolan dropped the transmission into gear and eased out into the street. Traffic was almost nonexistent. The bars and nightclubs around Vancouver were closing. The city was switching over from the clubs to the after-hours hangouts.

He turned right at the next intersection and scanned the traffic ahead. A dirty blue sedan rolled out of the street ahead. A cigarette coal glowed softly on the passenger side through the dark window. Four silhouettes marked the men inside the vehicle.

"The target should be within view," Price said.

"I have the target," Bolan said.

"There are two blockers, Striker. Both are in motion. Both emerged from the same building as the target."

The Executioner watched the side streets. Anyone running

in tandem with the sedan was going to stand out. "Affirmative. Two blockers. Have I got the money car?"

"Confirm that, Striker. You have the money car."

Bolan glanced at the three LAW 80 rocket launchers nestled into the passenger seat. The Ford Explorer was armored up and rolled on run-flat tires that would stay up and together even if they ran over spiked chain barricades. The destructive power of the LAW rockets gave the vehicle enough firepower to effectively be called a tank.

The money car was one of the vehicles the Moon Shadow triad used to collect the profits from their illegal businesses. Three times a week, the money cars rolled through Vancouver's streets, taking in the proceeds from the street drugs, prostitutes and small gambling casinos that operated throughout the city. From conservative estimates given by the Vancouver Asian Crime Task Force, the triad's money car usually carried upward of a half million dollars.

For most triads, a half million dollars might not be much. But for the Moon Shadow triad, cash poor from trying to start up legitimate businesses, a half million dollars was a lot to lose. Especially since the cash was already in the North American continent and didn't have to pass through customs.

"Blocker vehicles are running the side streets, Striker," Price said. "One up, one down."

"Acknowledged, Stony Base," Bolan replied. He kept behind the money car, trailing at a sedate pace behind the vehicle. The men in the car wouldn't want to be pulled over because their trunk was filled with cash. If found by a cop, the money would be seized, taken and the collection men deported or possibly jailed depending on what the Zhao family lawyers could do.

Bolan knew the route. Only five routes were taken through the city. Price had gleaned the information from the Carnation Building files that had been uploaded.

Hsiao, the security chief for the building, also managed the security for the pickups, coordinating the drops and the pickups through the computer. All of the information had been hidden through encryption coding, but Kurtzman's people took such things apart in their sleep.

The attack, Bolan knew, would be unexpected even though the men inside the vehicles had probably heard of the attacks on the Sports Fan Bar & Grill and the Carnation Building. The smart thing to have done would have been to lie low and leave the money for morning. Daylight pickups might have offered other challenges and dangers, but it would have been eight to twelve hours removed from the window of danger that had already proved open.

The Executioner spotted the intersection two blocks ahead. The street was four lanes wide. No one else traveled on it at the moment. Light traffic was only one of the reasons why the money car rolled this route. There were also many alleys to fade away into.

Slipping his hand under his duster, Bolan fisted the Beretta 93-R. He used the electric button on the driver's-side door panel to roll down the passenger-side window.

The glass smoothly disappeared into the door. Street noises, tires hissing against the pavement, belligerent drivers only a street or two over and the mournful wail of tugs working English Bay pushed into the Explorer.

Bolan pulled to the inside lane as if to pass the sedan.

Inside the car, the orange glow of the cigarette coal turned in Bolan's direction.

The Executioner kept his foot on the accelerator, maintaining the slightly faster pace than the sedan. When the man looked away again, Bolan lifted the Beretta and fired through the Ford's passenger-side window.

The bullet cored through the left rear tire. The tire deflated instantly. The money car's brake lights flared crimson as the back end shimmied on the flat tire.

The money car pulled to the right, less than forty yards short of the intersection.

Bolan slid smoothly by, lifting the Beretta again as he came even with the driver. He fired a round through the driver's head, killing him instantly in a burst of crimson that painted the inside of the windshield. All of the men in the money car were violent men. They'd killed in China and they'd killed in Canada.

The dead man's foot dropped onto the accelerator. The front tires shrilled as they burned rubber for an instant, then grabbed hold.

Bolan raised the passenger-side window and put his own foot down on the Explorer's accelerator. The huge power plant surged with renewed life and shoved the soldier back in the seat. He steered with his left hand, keeping the Beretta in his right.

When the Explorer leaped forward and overtook the money car, Bolan watched the men in the passenger seat and the back seat lunging for the steering wheel. He yanked his own wheel hard to the right, catching the sedan alongside and muscling it over to the right. Metal crunched and screamed.

A man in the back seat drew a pistol and blasted the Explorer from point-blank range. The steel-jacketed lead bounced harmlessly from the armor and the bulletproof windows but sounded like peals of thunder inside the vehicle.

Bolan again lowered the passenger window and shot the man, sending him over into the other man in the back seat. Chunks of safety glass spilled from the window. The Executioner yanked on the wheel again, using the Explorer's greater weight and size to overpower the sedan.

The sedan left the street and went up over the curb. A heartbeat later, the vehicle crunched into the side of the building and came to a sudden halt.

Bolan coasted on by. Metal shrilled as the Explorer slid

down the length of the sedan. Tapping the brake, Bolan pulled the Explorer around.

"Striker," Price called, "the two blocker cars are en route. The one coming from the north will reach you first."

Calm, knowing that taking the money car out of the play had been the chief objective and it had been completed, the Executioner grabbed the shoulder straps of the three LAW 80 rockets. He slipped out the door, looking to the north, then stepped to the side of the Explorer.

The soldier unlimbered one of the tubes, released the safeties to telescope the weapon's length and took up a position looking across the Explorer's hood. He steadied the LAW and curled his finger around the trigger, then waited.

The new arrival was another sedan. Four men occupied the vehicle. All of them were Chinese, and all of them carried pistols and submachine guns in plain sight now.

"Stony Base," Bolan stated, "confirm presence of secondary target."

"Secondary target confirmed, Striker. Target is right in front of you."

Bolan took up trigger slack. Inside the tube over his right shoulder, the rocket ignited, spitting flames. The 94 mm warhead leaped from the LAW launcher. The six spring-loaded stabilizing fins fanned out behind the warhead as it sped toward the sedan.

The HEAT explosive round impacted against the side of the car. The blast threw a scalding wave of heated air over Bolan's position, but it knocked the four men flat. Flames clawed the sedan, raking the vehicle with savage fury. One of the men tried to get up, but the flames caught the sedan's gas tank on fire, triggering another eruption that broke the sedan in two. Both pieces bounced across the street. None of the four passengers moved.

Bolan tossed away the spent LAW tube and readied the

next. The LAW 80s were totally fire-and-forget pieces of ordnance. Flames coiled from the burning vehicle, plucking at the shadows that covered the buildings from the night.

Catching movement from his peripheral vision, the Executioner turned and drew the Desert Eagle from his hip. As soon as the big Magnum pistol came level, he fired at the man who had stumbled from the back of the sedan pinned against the building.

The triad gunner had time to get off one brief burst from an Uzi before the .44 round caught him in the chest and punched him backward. The blood that spread across his shirtfront was mute testimony that he hadn't been wearing Kevlar.

"Striker," Price called, "the other secondary target is on you and coming fast."

Bolan heard the sedan coming. He twisted, trying to bring the second LAW to his shoulder, then saw that the approaching vehicle was too close and there was no time to get the shot off before the car was on him.

Muzzle-flashes sparked from the windows as the arriving car expertly spun sideways and slewed toward the Explorer.

Moving quickly, Bolan flung himself across the Explorer's hood. He rolled and landed on his feet, dropping into a crouch to use the SUV as cover. He holstered the Desert Eagle and grabbed one of the two LAW 80s hanging from his shoulder. Then the second blocker car slammed into the Explorer, carrying enough weight and speed to shove the big vehicle aside.

The Executioner sprawled, knocked ten feet by the impact. He managed to keep his grip on the LAW 80. Bullets pocked the street around him. He rolled to his side, staying ahead of the bullets, and saw the man's head and shoulders over the side of the Explorer. The guy was obviously hanging out the sedan's window, firing over and across the SUV's hood.

Still in motion, Bolan rolled and fired the LAW. The 94 mm

HEAT warhead spit from the tube and streaked across the short distance. Most of the high-intensity explosive blast was wasted against the Explorer's armored hide, but the direct hit on the gunman tore him to pieces. The concussive force shoved at Bolan, rocking him against the street.

Startled by the blast, the sedan driver put the pedal to the metal and roared away. The Explorer shook, knocking flaming pieces of corpse from the roof and hood.

Dazed but still responsive, Bolan stood and dragged the final LAW from his shoulder. He stood his ground, extended the tube and flipped the sights into position. When he'd locked on to his target, he fired.

The 94 mm warhead whooshed across the distance separating the soldier from the car. The blast lifted the car, turning the vehicle over to pancake on its roof. A moment later, the gasoline tank exploded, filling the sedan's interior with flames.

Tossing the empty tube away, knowing police investigators wouldn't be able to trace the weapons or whatever fingerprints he might have left on the equipment, Bolan turned his attention back to the money car. He filled his hand with the Desert Eagle.

Only the man in the passenger seat beside the dead driver remained alive. The gunner was dazed and badly injured from the crash against the building. Almost unconscious, blood trailing from his right cheekbone and the corner of his mouth, the man gazed up at Bolan.

"Tell Saengkeo Zhao that I want the nuclear weapon," the Executioner said in a graveyard voice. He slipped the key from the ignition. "Tell her that things will get worse for the Moon Shadows from this point on if I don't get the weapon. Tell her I'll be in touch."

"Who—who are you?" the man asked.

"She'll know me," Bolan said. With the keys in hand, he

walked to the back of the car, opened the trunk and removed the luggage containing the take the men had been hauling. Moving all the money took two trips.

He threw the cash into the Explorer, then climbed behind the wheel. The vehicle was damaged but not too badly to drive. Once he returned the Explorer to the safehouse, a crew would go to work on the vehicle. Either the Explorer would be repaired with new identification papers by morning, or it would be chopped to bits and shipped out on a freighter.

Bolan steered between the burning husks of the two blocker cars. He studied the wreckage strewed across the street behind him. The ball was in Saengkeo's court. The Executioner wanted to wait to see what she would do.

Los Angeles, California

SAENGKEO STARED at the CNN broadcast in shock. The media had already made the ties between the Sports Fan Bar & Grill and the Carnation Buildings. Now there was some speculation that an attack on three cars only moments ago was also somehow related to the Moon Shadow triad.

The knowledge made her almost physically ill. She knew her family maintained a criminal presence in Vancouver, but never had she seen that face painted onto them so blatantly. She and her brother, and their father before them, had worked long and hard to make Vancouver a safe and welcoming environment for the legitimate family businesses.

Only the presence of the other triads and the Chinese street gangs that would prey on them had prompted her father, then Syn-Tek, to keep a gangster force in the city. Now all their businesses, including the ones they had worked so hard to keep distant and separate from the criminal activities, would suffer suspicion. The Vancouver police would put those businesses under microscopes that would make day-to-day living for her people nearly unbearable.

The thought almost broke Saengkeo's heart. Her family had promised those people that they would be kept from the violence that now erupted around them. It wasn't fair.

"There will be repercussions from this," Johnny Kwan said at her side.

"I know," Saengkeo replied dully. There was precious little hope left within, and she felt that she faced imminent defeat. Even if she found the man in black, she knew she would have to have him killed to stop him. Even in Hong Kong a few days ago, she'd had to resort to the kind of upfront violence that she had promised herself she would stay away from.

"I need to go there," Kwan said.

Saengkeo looked away from the television to the man who had been her brother's best friend. Only Kwan's men were in the room, all of them alert and working security. Pei-Ling had retired to one of the bedrooms, and she'd gone off upset and angry, wanting Saengkeo to pursue her as she had when they were children. Saengkeo had felt none of the old inclinations.

"A statement must be made in Vancouver before things get worse," Kwan stated calmly. "The Moon Shadow family must go after this man."

"Only one man, Johnny? From the damage that was done tonight, you would think there must be a small army of men."

Kwan shook his head. "It is only one man. The same man we faced briefly on the Russian freighter." He nodded at the television where videotape from the Carnation Building and the Sports Fan Bar & Grill played. Kwan's men moved quickly when their master wanted results. "If you study him, study the way that he moves, you will know it is him."

"But who is he?"

"I don't know." Kwan looked back at her. "I don't trust this CIA agent, Stoddard. And I don't trust the American government. They all have their own agendas."

"And this man?" Saengkeo pointed her chin at the videotape footage. "What is his agenda?"

"He wants the nuclear weapons," Kwan said.

"But I don't know where the other one is."

"He thinks that you do. And he won't go away until he believes differently."

"Why would he want the weapons?"

Kwan shrugged. "Perhaps he has been hired by the people that the weapons were stolen from."

"You mean the Russian *mafiya*."

"Yes."

"Pei-Ling said this man was American."

A grimace tightened Kwan's face beneath the sunglasses. "Pei-Ling isn't an authority on nationalities."

"She knows men."

Kwan maintained a neutral expression. "If he was working for the Russians, he wouldn't have attacked their ship."

"If this man isn't working for the Russians," Saengkeo said, her mind grappling with all the possibilities, "he could be working for the Middle Eastern terrorist buyers."

"According to Stoddard, the terrorist group has already paid for the delivery of the weapons," Kwan pointed out.

"They have paid half the delivery price," Saengkeo said. "That isn't the same as paying full price. And if delivery isn't made, they can get their money back. Perhaps the terrorists agreed to the deal with the *mafiya* only to expose the weapons so they could get them." Such things had been done among the triads, and with those who had dealings with the triads.

"They would still have to pay this man's price." Kwan regarded the video footage. "Such a man wouldn't be cheap, and he wouldn't be driven to such lengths as to attack Moon Shadow holdings in Vancouver." He paused. "This man could be working for another triad."

That possibility hadn't occurred to Saengkeo. "Why would another triad hire someone to do this?"

"Another triad," Kwan stated flatly, "might view the Moon Shadows as being weak. For years, your father has been moving the family business into more legitimate pursuits."

"That was a promise my great-grandfather made." A flicker of anger passed through Saengkeo, but she quickly quelled the emotion. Johnny Kwan knew what had driven her family, and he had been a part of that design.

"The other triads don't care, Saengkeo. That is one thing I have always felt your family forgot—or simply chose to ignore."

The plain statement, if voiced by someone other than Johnny Kwan, would have been dealt with harshly. A triad leader couldn't afford to be questioned. In another triad, Kwan would have been slain outright or ostracized for daring to say anything that might be taken as criticism.

"There are triad leaders out there," Kwan said, "that waited for your father to fail. They waited for Syn-Tek to fail." He was quiet for the briefest moment. "And they wait for you to fail, Saengkeo. Like sharks that have the scent of blood in the water, they wait. When you fail, when you stumble, someone like Wei-Lim Yang will attempt to step in and take over your family."

Saengkeo regarded Johnny Kwan. His stare from behind the black-lensed sunglasses remained implacable, above reproach. "And do you think that one of them one day will succeed?"

He looked at her, his face set like stone. "Not as long as I yet live, Saengkeo Zhao. This I swear."

Saengkeo felt embarrassed and angry at herself. That simple question was as close as she'd ever come to questioning Johnny Kwan's loyalty. "I'm sorry," she said in a small voice.

"For what?"

"For insulting you."

A small smile twisted Kwan's lips. "You did not insult me."

Saengkeo started to speak, but Kwan continued before she could.

"To struggle with doubt and wish affirmation is the hardship of a leader," Kwan said. "The only way you could have insulted me was by asking someone else where I would stand should things become difficult for you. Or, perhaps, to doubt secretly and never ask me so that you could trust my word. Syn-Tek also asked me the same question."

Saengkeo was surprised.

"He asked me at your father's funeral," Kwan said. "Until Syn-Tek refused to let me go with him to recover the first nuclear weapon, I thought he trusted me implicitly."

"He did," Saengkeo said. "He left you behind because he was afraid that something would go wrong. If anything did, he wanted you here to help me."

"I know," Kwan said. "But knowing doesn't make losing him any easier."

"No."

"Don't try to figure this man out, Saengkeo." Kwan returned his attention to the video footage. "There is only one thing you must know and concentrate on in your dealings with him—he is your enemy. He has killed members of your family, and he has taken honor and respect from the Moon Shadows that only blood—his, that of others who will seek to prey on us because of this, and that of our family members who will pay the price for what has been done there today—will fix."

Saengkeo's heart ached with the weight of Kwan's words, but she knew they were true. The damage that had been dealt to the Moon Shadows extended much further than the loss of businesses, profits and the lives of the hardmen who had guarded those things. If she didn't get her operations in hand in Vancouver, she would lose more than those things. She would lose much of the future that her father, brother and she had been working on for their family.

More than anything, she wished she were back in Hong Kong, in the school where the children of her family went so that she could sit on the bench with Ea-Han. Surely he would have words of wisdom that would guide her. But she didn't like to involve the old man in the sordid aspects of the Moon Shadow triad's criminal business.

She turned to Kwan. "Something must be done."

Kwan nodded. "I'll make arrangements."

"For both of us," Saengkeo said.

Kwan started to say something, then stopped himself. A small smile twisted his lips. "Of course. I'll take care of it now."

After Kwan left her, Saengkeo remained staring at the television screen, watching as the man in black marched through the Carnation Building. The cameras kept him in view constantly, but the action was slightly blurred because he simply moved so fast. She watched as he herded women from one of the rooms. They were afraid of him, screaming and panicked, but he had never placed a hand upon them except to get them moving.

Why hadn't he killed some of the women? The question nagged at Saengkeo. A mercenary wouldn't have hesitated about killing anyone who fell into his sights. But the man in black had taken pains to be certain of his shots. Still, he had killed ruthlessly, a man who was very thorough in his business—and very deadly. The final numbers on the body count hadn't yet been decided.

Then she realized that the business had been the target. Not the people. Somehow the distinction was important, but the man couldn't possibly believe that she would react any differently because of it.

Perhaps, before she had him killed, Saengkeo would get the chance to ask.

* * * * *

Don't miss the exciting conclusion of
THE MOON SHADOW TRILOGY.
Look for The Executioner #298,
FINAL PLAY, in September.

James Axler
Outlanders

SEA OF PLAGUE

The loyalties that united the Cerberus warriors have become undone, as a bizarre messenger from the future provides a look into encroaching horror and death. Kane and his band have one option: fix two fatal fault lines in the time continuum—and rewrite history before it happens. But first they must restore power to the barons who dare to defy the greater evil: the mysterious new Imperator. Then they must wage war in the jungles of India, where the deadly, beautiful Scorpia Prime and her horrifying bio-weapon are about to drown the world in a sea of plague....

In the Outlands, the shocking truth is humanity's last hope.

Stony Man is deployed against an armed
invasion on American soil...

AXIS OF
CONFLICT

The free world's worst enemy failed to destroy her once
before, but now they've regrouped and expanded—a jihad
vengeance that is nothing short of bio-engineered
Armageddon, brilliant and unstoppable. A weapon unlike
anything America has ever seen is about to be unleashed on
U.S. soil. Stony Man races across the globe in a desperate
bid to halt a vision straight out of doomsday—with
humanity's extinction on the horizon....

STONY
MAN

*Available in
August 2003
at your favorite
retail outlet.*

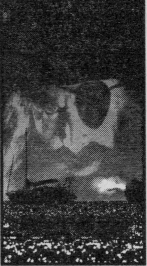

DEATH LANDS.®

Devil Riders

*Available in September 2003
at your favorite retail outlet.*

Stranded in the salty desert wastes of West Texas, hopes for a hot meal and clean bed in an isolated ville die fast when Ryan and his companions run into a despotic baron manipulating the lifeblood of the desert: water. But it's his fortress stockpiled with enough armaments to wage war in the dunes that interests Ryan, especially when he learns the enemy may be none other than the greatest—and long dead—Deathlands legend: the Trader.

Or order your copy now by sending your name, address, zip or postal code, along with a check or money order (please do not send cash) for $6.50 for each book ordered ($7.99 in Canada), plus 75¢ postage and handling ($1.00 in Canada), payable to Gold Eagle Books, to:

In the U.S.	In Canada
Gold Eagle Books	Gold Eagle Books
3010 Walden Ave.	P.O. Box 636
P.O. Box 9077	Fort Erie, Ontario
Buffalo, NY 14269-9077	L2A 5X3

Please specify book title with order.
Canadian residents add applicable federal and provincial taxes.

GOLD
EAGLE®

GDL63

James Axler
Outlanders®

AWAKENING

Cryogenically preserved before the nukes obliterated their own way of life, an elite team of battle-hardened American fighting men has now been reactivated. Their first mission in a tortured new world: move in and secure Cerberus Redoubt and the mat-trans network at any cost. In a world where trust is hard won and harder kept, Kane and his fellow exiles must convince Team Phoenix that they are on the same side—for humanity, and against the hybrids and their willing human allies.

In the Outlands, the shocking truth is humanity's last hope.